BONA FIDE STREET THUG

A novel by
Donald Ray Johnson

Second Edition

Southern Classic Publishing
Mansfield, Texas

Southern Classic Publishing, L.L.C.

990 Hwy 287 N Ste 106 #298

Mansfield, Texas 76063

Office: 682-587-9818

www.southernclassicpublishing.com

Bona Fide Street Thug

Second Edition

ISBN 13-digit 978-0-9915814-0-5

Library of Congress Control Number: 2014903494

Library of Congress Cataloging-in-Publishing Data   Donald Ray Johnson, African-American, Contemporary, Urban Crime, Houston, Texas – Fiction

Edited by Mary McBeth, www.UrbanFictionEditor.com
Layout and Interior Design by: UrbanFictionMedia.com
Cover by Oddball Design

Dedication

To my sister Tameshia Kay Johnson, and to my daddy, Mr. Arthur Irvin Johnson. Sister, I know your spirit watches over me. You will always be in my memories. We love and miss you dearly. Old man, you was real all the way to the end. I never got the chance to say goodbye before you left, but I will always remember you and your favorite saying, "Patience is a Virtue." Rest in Peace!

Acknowledgements

First and foremost, I'd like to give praise to our Heavenly Father for creating such fine species of both men and women.

Without Him, many things would not be possible and He has given me the knowledge I need to be super-successful, strong, patient and totally dominant. He helped me see life in this world for what it really is and I say unto Him, thanks for being there for me and all my loved ones.

Mama - Mrs. Thelma Betties - you are the most precious person I know. You stood by me when no one else would. You are strong, supportive and, above all, faithful. I love you dearly and I truly cherish the time we have left on this earth together. I love you, mama!

To my wife LaChandra - You came to me when I was at my lowest point and stood by me all the way to the top. You watched as I turned my potential into prosperity and learned about a love you thought never existed. I appreciate you, your kind heart and, most of all, your patience. I love you, baby, and that's 100%.

To my younger brother, Cardell (aka "Man-Man"), and Kendra, my niece, Icy Olivia and sisters Tonya and Kim. I thank you all for always looking up to me. I love all y'all.

Special Thanks

Mary McBeth, Ms. Super-cool! I thank you for all your knowledge and the insight you gave us on the company business. Your skills are definitely above average and we're honored to have a relationship with such a talented individual. To my critics: Samuel "Shakur" Lee, James "4" Alexander, Tommy Jr., Michael "New York" Lykes, Bobby D. Punch (wud up boy), Southwest Pat Broadnax, my boys Zeik and Ralph "N.O." Mitchell, Michael Oats(fats), Cedric "Itty Bitty" Johnson (Southside still holdin'), San Antonio Cain, Michael Dupree (D-Town), Hood, 5th Ward Reece, my potna Torrence "Magic" Samuels, Demetrius Johnson (keep ya head up, homey) and thanks for all the insight, Linus Johnson (44 Acres Homes), Russell Leonard, my boy Jay Davis (44 Acres Homes) and many more. It was these cats who inspired me to put it down and get this book into print. I appreciate that, fellas.

Dear Readers,

This series represents an exciting, most tale-thriving opportunity for me to incorporate your feedback on this new favorably loved street story. If you have heard of this story, or perhaps you have not, and have gotten the chance to get your hands on it, then I hope to fascinate and captivate you with the intriguing life of a "Bona Fide Street Thug". In this novel, you will see what is relevant on the streets of Houston, Texas. I kept the action original, poured on the street flavor and mixed in a couple of sex scenes for your own personal entertainment. You will be thirsty for more and anxious to read Street Work, the second novel of the Bona Fide Street Thug series. After you get into the third book please provide your feedback, because my goal was to make these stories as compelling and entertaining enough to be heartfelt. Now I honestly have to tell you that, as an author, this series has been a blast to write and I thoroughly enjoyed writing it for you. Each book is a wonderful challenge; all loaded with suspense and intensely felt. You will understand some of the things that actually happen on the streets and the characters will grow on you as the story unfolds. So stay tuned, check the websites regularly and send in your comments. I take time to consider every letter. Your feedback is important. This series comes straight from my experiences, and with your support I will continue to bring you the style of writing you enjoy. I hope I've done that with this one. Enjoy!

-Donald Ray Johnson

Introduction

What is the true definition of a Bona Fide Street Thug? Well, when you really look at it, there are many ways you can define this character. You can call him a pimp, a hustler, a jacker, a drug dealer, a gangster, a player or whatever you want to call him, but a true Bona Fide Street Thug is the type of guy who can put his hands into anything on the streets. His style is genuine and his moves are those of a mastermind. All-in-all, this is your every day, average guy who gets up in the morning and puts on his pants just like any other person. Careful, though, this every day, average guy is not one you should take so lightly. Hi, my name is Donald Ray Johnson and I'm about to tell you the story of a guy named Javoo.

Prologue

Javoo lived in the heart of Southpark with his 5' foot 9" yellow-bone fiancé Tanasia, and two kids. Their spot was located not too far from an elementary school and dead-center of a crack infested neighborhood. He'd kept a nice stash of money at all times, which was his reason for having 2 pit-bull dogs in his backyard that dared any uninvited guest to step foot inside his back gate.

He knew the streets and he definitely knew his own hood. He knew boys didn't play. It didn't matter if you were a chump or a Baller. Your best homey or even your next door neighbor would run up in yo' spot if they knew you had the kinda bread he had layin' around. That was just how dirty some people were and he knew he was one of 'em.

His car was a smooth looking '96 SS Impala that sat on a chrome set of 22" inch rims and Pirelli tires, a black paint job with black leather interior. He didn't have a job to go to like some of the other fellas on his block. Meanwhile, his fiancé barely managed to hold onto the job she hated so much, working at a nursing home, changing old shitty diapers of the elderly and passing out medication, while her girlfriends went out to the clubs almost every night. But still, it paid the bills, along with what Javoo had to offer, and she didn't know where or how it was that he managed to come up with the type of

1

money that he did. She knew he sold drugs or at least he once did. But he was gone so much her thoughts of his money-making were totally indescribable.

Turning corners in his Impala, Javoo peeped the scenes of the local night spots. Carringtons, Reminisce and Breakers: they would all be his pattern. Not necessarily having a specific place to go, he would sometimes see a homey or a relative and make his stop, which led to the pouring of a special drink they called "syrup", or smoking some exotic brand of hydro marijuana.

He was always on the hunt for a new come-up, as he watched how the Carringtons parking lot, busy like ants, would be stylish and very competitive. Sometimes he would short-stop a couple of jazzy-looking college cuties who were out on the town and looking to get into something or go for the sexiest chick in the club just to high-side on some of his homies. That was his style. His swagger would always win him a phone number or two, but his conversation, the way he dressed and what he was riding in would award him with much more most of the time.

He played no games when it came to getting' money and having a conversation with his homey, Cornelius; after he'd downloaded another dime piece's number into his phone, it really gave him something to smile about. Armed with a plastic issue Glock 17-9mm, with an infra-red beam, Javoo would be ready for whatever went down and Cornelius had just given him the perfect scheme for the evening.

They drove towards the southwest side of town as Javoo spoke on his cell, to a female associate, about a money order scam that would go down first thing in the morning. That was just the white-collar side of the game. Jackin', hittin' for major licks, was his main thing and as they turned into the parking lot of a shell station, there awaited a girl named Chitora "Chi-Chi" Hastings, whom Cornelius had met one beautiful Sunday at Herman Park.

She was his girlfriend. She was jazzy, single, had no kids and had not too long ago inherited some money after her parents had been killed in a train accident up in Jersey. She had bread. They knew her as the sister of a high-roller named Ralph, who had been making his mark in Houston as a business man and a drug dealer. But Chi-Chi, unaware of what was going to happen, only wanted Cornelius to come and spend the evening with her while she babysat for her brother and his wife, who were planning to go to a concert. They wanted to rob Ralph, and Javoo's plan would be a beast, as he pretended to only drop Cornelius off, but then circle around and follow them at a safe and unnoticeable distance. Once Cornelius and Chi-Chi were inside the house and when the time was right, he used his cell phone as a signal for Javoo to invade the home.

Cornelius, who was a few years younger than Javoo, would seem to be only a young kid to Chi-Chi's brother, but his gun-play would also be vicious. He really did like Chi-Chi, but he had grown up in the slums of 3rd Ward, The Trey, and needed money badly. He just wasn't tryin' to hear it, and when Ralph and his wife Donna came downstairs, Cornelius made the call and Javoo sprang into action, drawing down on everyone in the house.

3

Chi-Chi was crushed. She couldn't believe that Cornelius would do such a thing. A life that she never knew of had been riding with her the whole time. Tears began to roll from her eyes, as they duct taped her and began to interrogate her brother for the combination to his safe. She thought that Javoo was going to kill him, the way he had his gun pressed down hard on Ralph's head. But Ralph cooperated. He didn't want to die and he didn't want no one else to die either. He knew he had plenty of money in the bank - legal money - so he told them whatever they wanted to know and watched as they walked out the front door of his home with his own personal stash.

That night, Javoo and Cornelius had won for $75,000 in cash from Ralph's safe, 3 kilos of cocaine they'd found in the closet inside a shopping bag, and around $20,000 in jewelry. This took them to a place where they could split their come-up and then go in their own direction for the evening.

Pulling into his driveway, Javoo thought of how Cornelius always looked up to him and how they both made the decision about the money they had just made. He knew Cornelius would be a little shaken up about what he had done to his own girlfriend, but it was tough out on the streets and he wanted his young homey to get on his feet and stay on his feet. He took only $35,000, 2 kilos, and under $5,000 worth of jewelry, which would definitely be a nice addition to the stash he already had.

His two kids were sound asleep while Tanasia lay in bed with the night lamp on, reading an urban novel. She could never sleep as long as Javoo was gone, for she loved him so

4

much, she feared that he wouldn't come home because of the lust for another woman or trouble he could get into with the police. But Javoo, walking through the bedroom door broad and very much wide awake from the nights' adventure, would kiss her and then meddle her about staying up so late, knowing her feelings for him.

He sat sideways on the bed next to her and began to roll himself a blunt while she talked to him about his son, who was having problems at school. After a few minutes had passed, he went out into his backyard to check on his dogs and as he looked up into the sky, stars shining bright on him, he took a drag, blew out some smoke and smiled, for Javoo knew he was a Bona Fide Street Thug.

Chapter One

Three Years Later.

Standing 6' foot 1", wearing an all-black Kenneth Cole shirt and pants and sporting a pair of Gucci sun shades, Javoo stood near a small indoor-outdoor cafe in the Greenway Plaza area just outside of downtown Houston. His attention was directed to a 15-story sky-rise apartment building across the street, from where he awaited a female friend who was visiting a girlfriend to gain some information on a guy named Mitchell, the female's boyfriend. Javoo really didn't know the guy and on the cool, he really didn't want to. He just wanted his money. It was already understood that he was a local hustler and had been making a substantial amount of cash lately.

All he needed to know was where he kept his stash. He knew that the guy didn't live there, or at least keep anything there, after talking to his female friend, Shalon. She would always speak about how square her girlfriend Tracy was, and how Mitchell would brag about the money he was making. She had even told him about how he would always try to holla at her behind his girl's back, which was why he'd decided to go on and get him for his money. It wasn't that he was jealous of Mitchell or anything like that. He had plenty of his own bread.

It was just that jackin' was his full time job, and Mitchell was one that just so happened to make his own self his newest victim.

Mitchell was a local hustler indeed, though he purchased all his drugs across town from a guy named Money Black, whom Javoo once had a confrontation with. Money Black was ruthless, notorious, did a lot of high-cappin' and, most of all, considered himself as the King of the Northside. That was what had caused him and Javoo to get into it in the first place. He thought he could just come to any club in the south and show the Southside playaz up. That was until he bumped into Javoo and then tried to talk down on him like he was nothin'. That's when Javoo slapped him and then dropped him in front of two of his potnas, and ever since then they had not liked each other.

Javoo, whispering to himself and thinking of how Shalon would always get caught up in the small talk, was ready to split. He didn't want to incidentally get spotted by Mitchell and mess up his plans to hit him. Suddenly, the glass door of the building slowly opened and Shalon stepped out, locking eyes with him and saying in a low tone, "I'm comin', I'm comin'" as she crossed the street. Shalon was a 5' foot 6" dark-skinned chick who always wore something similar to a sundress and heels. She always carried a top name handbag, whether it was Gucci, Louis Vuitton, or a purse made by Dior or Prada. Her walk was out of this world and horns blew in appreciation of her. Not because she was in the street, but because of the way she so graciously scaled the surface over to where Javoo was standing.

"Ready to go?" Shalon asked. "Yeah, I was ready 20 minutes ago. I started to leave yo' ass," he said in a joking manner. "And if you would've ... ," Shalon said as they both walked towards the car. Javoo owned several rides, but would always purchase a rental for undercover moves he was going to make. He knew only a fool would rob somebody in his own vehicle and in Houston, Texas, that was a sure way to get your head busted. Shalon gave Javoo all the info that he needed on Mitchell as they headed towards the southwest side of town to where she lived. He'd stopped at a Timmy Chan's restaurant so that she could pick up a bite to eat and then swiftly drove to her apartment.

"You comin' in or what?" she asked as Javoo smiled softly.

"Not right now, lil' mama. I'll be back later," he said as she smacked her lips, got out and stompishly walked to her front door. He knew she wanted to have sex with him, for she was one of his favorites, but he had robbing Mitchell on his mind and wanted to show him just how watchful the streets are. He reached for his cell phone and dialed Cornelius's number, one of his most trusted homeys and partner in crime.

"Wud up?" Cornelius asked as soon as he answered.

"Meet me at Papadeaux on the 610 freeway. I'll be sitting at the bar," said Javoo.

"What's the deal? We got business or what?" Cornelius asked him.

"I thought you knew," said Javoo.

"Okay, see you in fifteen," Cornelius said and then hung up.

9

* * *

Mitchell had two things going for him. One, he was good looking, so he always had a ring of nice looking, independent women on his team. Two, he had gained the trust of Money Black, who would always make sure that he got his product. Mitchell handled 8 to 10 kilos of cocaine, at least 5 pounds of meth, and up to 75 pounds of hydro marijuana once every two weeks. He pretty much had the Richmond/Westheimer area sewed up, and had been a smooth operator with his business.. He had a quiet and cozy looking bachelor pad just off the Richmond strip, where he didn't allow anyone except his highest paid female friends and, sometimes, maybe a spur of the moment freak he would meet around the way. It was his hide-a-way, his place for comfort and also the nest for his product.

Stepping out of his Mercedes S550 as his garage door came shut, Mitchell walked into his condo and went to the kitchen, opened the fridge, grabbed a beer and popped the top.

"Aaahhh!" was the sound he made after taking a deep swallow. He had been thinking about his girlfriend, Tracy, and how madly in love she was with him. He had been using her account as another way to put up some of his street money and figured that someday he may marry her. But before he did, he wanted to get at her sexy ass friend, Shalon.

"Let me call this bitch," he said as he flopped down on the couch. He searched through his cell phone, found her number and waited for her to answer.

"Hello?" Shalon said as she answered. "What it do baby? What's happenin' witcha?" he asked her.

"Baby! Who is this? I think you got the wrong number," she said.

"It's ya boy, Mitchell. You know who this is," he said. Shalon was surprised that he had called her. She didn't know what to think, especially after what she had just done for Javoo.

"I thought that Tracy was your baby, and how did you get my number anyway?" she asked him.

"I got it from the caller ID," he told her.

"Ooooh! You ain't no good, tryin' to holla at me behind Tracy's back," Shalon said to him.

"Well, I didn't call to talk to you about Tracy; I called to talk to you," he said.

"Well, I'm about to take a bath, so you gon' have to call me back," said Shalon.

"Okay, I'll call you back in about an hour," said Mitchell.

"Bye, nigga," Shalon said and hung up.

* * *

Javoo and Cornelius sat at the bar flirting with three of the sexiest looking women in the restaurant. They sipped on Patron and cranberry, while two of the women sipped on Grey Goose and Red Bull, and the other a Jose Cuervo Gold chill shot with salt around the rim of the glass. They had planned on discussing how they were going to rob Mitchell, but were distracted when the three beautiful ladies showed up. Their conversation was just beginning to get quite interesting when Javoo's phone suddenly begin to ring.

"Excuse me ladies, I gotta take this call," he said as he stepped off to the end of the bar.

"What's up?" he said answering his phone.

"You wouldn't believe who just called me," said Shalon.

"I don't know…who?" he asked.

"That nigga, Mitchell," said Shalon.

"Whatchu mean, he just called you?" Javoo asked her.

"I told you he been tryin' to holla at me behind Tracy's back. He said he got my number from her caller ID," she said.

—

"Uh huh! You probably gave him your number," said Javoo.

"I didn't!" cried Shalon.

"Well, he callin' you and shit. Who's ho' is you, mine or his?" Javoo said mean-like.

"I ain't no ho'," Shalon replied.

"Well, you know what I'm tryin' to do. You trippin' talkin' to the nigga and shit," Javoo said.

"That's why I called you, cause I told him that I was about to take a bath, so he said he was gon' call me back in an hour," she told him.

"Okay, I'll be over there in a few minutes," Javoo said and then hung up. Javoo and Cornelius cut the chit-chat with the females short, got their numbers and left. They had a mission to complete, and Cornelius was thinkin' numbers as he followed him over to Shalon's apartment. "So what's up,? Talk to me," Cornelius said once they parked and got out. "This nigga just called Shalon sayin' that he got her number off his girl's caller ID," Javoo told him.

"Do he know you?" asked Cornelius.

"Nah, he don't know who I am, but let's talk inside," Javoo said as they walked to Shalon's front door. Javoo had a key to Shalon's apartment, but before he could find it on his key ring, she had already swung the door open.

"Hey Shalon," Cornelius said as they walked into her place. "Y'all want something to drink?" she asked, seeing that there was a certain serious look on Javoo's face.

"Nah, we cool," he said. When Mitchell called back, Javoo and Cornelius listened as she talked to him on the phone. They had a plan for him, and Javoo was always known to be a fast thinker, since his earlier plan would now have to be readjusted.

"Okay, this is what we gon' do," Javoo said once Shalon hung up the phone. He had already gotten Shalon to get the directions and the number to Mitchell's condo. He also gave her specific orders to go on over to his place while they followed her in a rental and would be fairly unnoticeable. He just felt that Mitchell thought he was too slick for his own good by allowing Shalon, his girl's best friend, to come to his spot on a spur. However, he also had to understand the safety of her reputation, and not let Mitchell think she knew of anything that was going to happen. He had told her to go in and talk casually as always, do a little flirting and comment on his and Tracy's relationship to stretch out the situation but, at the same time, not let him touch her and do the things he wanted, without making him sweat.

Cornelius quickly whispered to Javoo as they sat in the car and waited for a signal from Shalon. That was the best part about the whole move. Perfection!

"This is too easy. You think the nigga that stupid?" he asked him.

"Pussy is a motherfucka, plus Shalon a bad bitch. He'll do whatever she want him to do, as long as she ain't tryin' to leave," Javoo said as a smile spread on Cornelius's face.

Mitchell opened his door and let Shalon in. He couldn't believe he had actually gotten her to come over. He quickly offered her something to drink and then sat closely next to her, but Shalon did her best to stall him. She had to think of a way to get Javoo and Cornelius into that condo without Mitchell noticing. He had been touching and feeling all on her and, so, since she supposedly had already taken a bath, she insisted on him taking a shower before they did anything. That was all she had to say to get him out the way so that she could signal Javoo, and unbuttoning her pants had made her very persuasive. Mitchell knew it was on then, and jumped and ran upstairs to turn on the shower.

"Can I turn on some music?" Shalon yelled up to him as she heard him scramble around upstairs.

"Yeah, go ahead," Mitchell shouted. Shalon quickly called Javoo and went and unlocked the door once the music was on. As soon as Mitchell stepped in the shower, Javoo and Cornelius eased into the condo and lightly duct-taped Shalon. She didn't know that this was gon' be a part of the plan and trembled as she watched Javoo creep up stairs with a ski mask on and his gun in his hand.

"You gon' be straight. Javoo knows what he's doin'," Cornelius whispered to her. Seconds later Mitchell, with Javoo's hand clutched tightly to a belt around his neck and a gun pointed at his head, came downstairs. Javoo caught him just as he was getting out the shower, and Mitchell was as naked as a jaybird.

"You know what time it is, playa," Javoo said to him. Mitchell saw Shalon with her hands tied behind her back and tears coming from her eyes. A guy wearing a mask and holding a gun was standing over her and that's when he knew what was happening.

"Get down on the floor by yo' bitch, nigga," Javoo said as he slammed Mitchell to the floor and pressed his gun to Mitchell's head. Cornelius quickly came and began to duct tape him as well.

"Where that work at, nigga?" Javoo roughly asked him.

"Whatchu talkin' bout man, what work?" asked Mitchell. Javoo kicked him in his side and then slapped him on his naked ass as he kneeled down next to him.

"Whatchu think, I'm just visiting, nigga? I'ma blow this ho' brains all over yo' ass if you don't spit it out, ho' ass nigga," Javoo barked. Mitchell thought about what was happening. He had never been in a situation like this before. He knew he didn't want to die, and he sure as hell didn't want to be responsible for Shalon's death, not in his condo. "Upstairs...upstairs in the closet," he said as Javoo stood over him.

"Anyone of 'em move, you know what to do," Javoo said as he headed back to the stairway. Mitchell closed his eyes and shook his head from side to side, as he thought about the money he had stashed upstairs.

"This is fucked up," he said as he heard Shalon constantly speaking in a low tone, "Please don't kill me, please don't kill me."

"Shut up, nigga!" Cornelius ordered, just as Javoo came back downstairs carrying two large duffle bags. Mitchell began to wiggle around on the floor, as if he was gon' try to stop Javoo and Cornelius from leaving with the duffle bags. That's when Cornelius kicked him upside his head and then kneeled down to put his gun to his head.

"Keep yo' ho' ass still or I'm gon' bust you in yo' ass, nigga. You lucky we lettin' yo' ass live as it is, so you just lay right here and think about that," Cornelius said and then he and Javoo stepped out of the condo and quickly walked to the car. They drove down Richmond Avenue and then over to the 59 freeway. Cornelius had a jazzy little apartment there, in a place called Holly Hall, out on the south side of town and that's where they went to separate their win for the day. It was just a common thing to hit a nice lick and then go chill for the rest of the evening. They had just put in a full day's work and, thanks to Mitchell, the rest of the week wasn't going to look too bad either.

"Let's do this real quick, 'cause Tanasia been callin' me all day," Javoo said as he unzipped one of the duffle bags and then the other. Inside one of the duffle bags were five kilos of cocaine, a pound and a half of meth, and six pounds of Orange Cush hydro marijuana.

"Man, this cush smells good," Cornelius said pressing one of the huge Zip-locks to his nose.

"Yeah, but I bet it don't smell as good as this," Javoo said, showing Cornelius the money inside the other duffle bag. Javoo dumped the money onto the table and after 30 minutes had passed they were at $127,000 and still counting.

"This boy been puttin' in some work," Javoo said after counting his last stack.

"Where you at?" he asked Cornelius.

"This twenty one Gee's right here," he said as he pointed at a couple stacks of money.

"Whatchu got?" he asked him back.

"I got seventeen more right here. So, that's one sixty five altogether," Javoo said to him. Javoo had planned to give Shalon $25,000 for her part in the scam once she got back to her apartment. He took in $90,000 since he had planned the whole thing, had the rental, and Shalon, the key to Mitchell's condo.

Cornelius, he wasn't trippin' at all. He took in $50,000, three kilos of cocaine, the pound and a half of meth and three pounds of cush.

"I gotta go," Javoo said as he tucked his two bricks and three pounds of cush in with his money, gave Cornelius some dap and walked to the door. Now, he was just hoping that Shalon would get out of Mitchell's condo without getting hurt.

"You be careful and make sure you keep your phone on, " he said to Cornelius, then turned and walked to his car.

Chapter Two

Mitchell and Shalon both struggled as they wrestled with the duct tape that was tied around their wrists and ankles. They had never been tied down before and it was quite confusing for them to try to figure out what had just happened. For Mitchell, he didn't have any idea who those mask wearing haters were and he seriously wondered how they knew what he had stashed in his condo and where he lived. Shalon, on the other hand, was wondering why Javoo had come and did what he did, and then just left her there to fend for herself. She really liked him a lot and had always said that she would do anything for him, but never in-a million guesses would have thought she would've done something like this.

"Can you get up?" Mitchell asked Shalon. Shalon was very flexible and could rollover backwards onto her knees and then to her feet.

"There's a knife in one of the drawers in the kitchen. Try and get it," he said as he continued to struggle. Shalon hopped like a bunny rabbit to the kitchen, opened the drawer and reached for a knife. Back and forth she drove the knife through the tough duct tape until her arms sprang apart from behind her back. Then she cut the tape from around her ankles, thinking to herself how she was going to let Javoo have it for this stunt.

"Hurry up and cut me loose, dammit!" Mitchell angrily said. Shalon went over and began to cut his hands free, telling him how she could just stab him for getting her caught up in his mess.

"First Tracy, and then a gun pointed at my head. I should kill you myself," she said trying to keep him thrown off of her having anything to do with the robbery.

"I'm leavin' before I get killed, fuckin' witchu nigga. And don't call me no more," she said as she grabbed her purse and walked out the door.

For the moment, Shalon really wasn't his main concern. He still owed Money Black $55,000 for some product he had gotten from him a few days earlier. He'd thought that he could knock down Shalon and soon after go and payoff Money Black, but his plans to do that had been spoiled by two unknown masked men. He was still wondering who they were and, most of all, how he was going to get back the money he had just lost. He hated to lose money, whether it was a dollar or a hundred dollars, but a hundred and sixty five thousand - that was a helluva loss and he needed to talk to somebody about what had just happened. That's when he picked up his phone and called Money Black.

"I was wondering when you was gon' call me," Money Black said as soon as he answered. "We gotta meet right now. I need to talk to you," Mitchell said to him.

"You got that bread or what?" Money Black asked him.

"Man, I just got robbed, but I don't wanna talk to you about it over the phone," he said.

Money Black had Mitchell to meet him at a corner store, just down the street from his car and accessories shop. He didn't know what to expect, being that Mitchell told him he had just got robbed. All he knew was that the jackers could be following him to find out who he was gettin' his work from - either them or the police. Either way, he didn't want to take no chance by letting him come directly to the shop.

Money Black was all the way low key. Nobody knew where he really lived, except only his younger brother C-Dub and maybe his grandmother. He was known to sometimes hang out at the Harlem Knights strip club during the week or maybe at Club Onyx, but that was about it. He moved at least 40 birds and up to 300 pounds of hydro marijuana a week. He owned a beauty and barber shop, a clothing store in a shopping center that was raking in some decent cash and, of course, a car and accessories shop. He had been doing his thang for the last five years and wasn't hurting for any money, but $55,000 was $55,000 and he wanted his money.

He watched as Mitchell pulled up in his black Mercedes, stepped out, and then got in on the passenger side of his 750 BMW. He just had to listen to his excuse as to why he didn't have his money.

"Now what happened?" he asked as Mitchell began to shake his head from side to side. Mitchell went on to tell him how two masked men invaded his condo and duct taped him while they searched his place. He also explained to him how he could get his girl Tracy to go to the bank tomorrow morning to get the money that he owed him.

"So you're tellin' me that two dudes just kicked your door in?" Money Black said as he began to drill Mitchell. Mitchell just shook his head.

"Where were you when they came in?" he asked.

"I was in the shower," he replied. Money Black was far from being dumb. He knew that two people wouldn't just run up in his spot, not knowing if he was in the shower or not, and he wasn't tryin' to hear nothing about no perfect timing.

"You must of had a freak in the shower with you?" he asked, knowing that Mitchell didn't hardly go a day without hooking up with a female and he felt that he was leaving out something. "Well, I did have this chick over; she got duct taped, too," Mitchell said in an ashamed tone of voice. "Then you need to check that ho' out, nigga, 'cause didn't that seem to be all too perfect? Now get out of my car and get me my money," Money Black said in a boss-like tone. Mitchell frowned as he got out of Money Black's car and back into his own. His thoughts were all over Shalon, so he picked up his cell phone and speed dialed her number. He wasn't getting an answer and so he tried the number again and again.

"B-I-T-C-H!" he yelled inside his car and then slammed his phone down into the console, after hearing her answering service pick up for the third time. He was thinking to himself that maybe she was still mad at him about what went down earlier, but then he didn't know where she lived and so he had to get an answer. He reached for his phone and tried the number once more, but couldn't get Shalon to pick up. Then he thought about his girl Tracy. He had to go and talk to her about going to the bank first thing in the morning. He had been getting her to make some pretty nice deposits for him lately, and he was glad, too. She had always told him that he blew too much money and insisted on putting some of it in her account for safe keeping. Still, he needed to come up with a way to get in touch with Shalon or at least try to talk Tracy into telling him where she lived without giving her any indication that he had tried to sleep with her friend.

Chapter Three

Javoo sat back in his favorite recliner and flipped through the channels on the plasma big screen, while his son Javon nagged at his daughter Natasia.

"Daddy, tell Javon to stop," his daughter cried out after his son had grabbed one of her dolls by the hair.

"Leave her alone, kid," he said in a calm tone, not even looking in their direction. His wife Tanasia stood in the kitchen preparing a dinner plate for him.

"I'm gon' whoop yo' ass boy if you don't stop!" she yelled to their son from the kitchen. She had seemed to be a little snappy since Javoo stepped in the door. She had already fussed at him about wherever he had been and now she was yelling at their son from across the dining room. But she was the woman of the house, so blowing off a little steam was normal and it always tickled him, because he knew that she wasn't going to be upset with him for too long.

"Here you go, baby," she said as she brought Javoo his plate and then went back to get some hot sauce and punch to go with his meal. Tanasia was an excellent cook, coming from a family of three sisters and four brothers. She was next to the youngest, so she had spent a lot of time watching her mom cook and clean as she came up. She had just recently quit the nursing home job she worked for three and a half years to go and open the Best Wishes Children's Center, a very well-organized and appreciated day care that Javoo funded just after they were married. She had an Alicia Keys-type of appeal in the sense when you looked at her, by her skin tone and the way that she wore her hair. She was beautiful.

"Are you going anywhere else tonight?" she asked Javoo as he sat back with both of his jaws full of food. "Look at you starving to death," she cracked at him with a smile on her face.

"I haven't ate nothin' all day," he said and then took a sip of his drink. "And yes, I do have a run I need to make," he said as she rolled her eyes at him and headed towards their bedroom. Javoo had a five foot safe in one of the closets that only he knew the combination to. She had seen him work the small knob to the safe, unlocked it and then placed a large duffle bag on top of it, so she thought that his day was finally over. She hated the fact that he did what he did, whatever that was, but he was coming in with lots and lots of money. She rarely asked him where he was going or where he was gettin' it from; she just wanted him to come home.

It was now 8:30pm and Javoo had Shalon on his mind, more so than Mitchell did. He had been thinking to himself of how she had better found a way to get out of Mitchell's condo and having to hear that someone had to pack her out was something he couldn't imagine.

"Hope she made it," he said as he put his plate in the kitchen sink and then pulled out his cell phone to call Cornelius. "Hey, what's up?" Cornelius said as he answered. "Call Shalon and see if she made it home safe for me, okay? 'Cause I'm here at the house," Javoo quickly said, trying not to let Tanasia hear him.

"I gotcha," Cornelius said and then hung up. Javoo stepped into his bedroom, where Tanasia sat sideways on their bed. He went over to try and kiss her, but she faked-like she didn't want him to touch her.

"Don't act like that, Baby," he said as he grabbed her and hugged her. "Stop, Javarius! You been in the streets all day. Can't you stay at home with us sometimes?" she asked as she looked at him.

"Baby, don't give me no hard time, okay? You know everything that I do is for us," he said as he stood and walked to the closet that the safe was in.

He pulled the door open, grabbed the duffle bag and started transferring money from the bag to the safe. Tanasia's eyes widened at the sight of all the stacks of money in the safe. She couldn't believe her eyes. The safe was nearly filled to the top and from back to front. She watched as he took $25,000 and sat it to the side and then listened as he talked to her about depositing the money into their bank. One of her girlfriends was a bank manager, so she was always able to deposit unusually large amounts of cash into their account without question. He had a little over one million dollars put into the bank over the last past 9 months and was now sitting on another $400,000 plus in his safe.

"You need to do something about Javon. He's starting to act just like you. He won't listen, he's been acting up at school and I'm tired of his teacher callin' me 'cause he won't shut up and do his work. You need to start spending some time with him," Tanasia said as Javoo cut her off.

"I do spend time with him," he said, seeming angry at what she was saying.

"Don't you know that he watches everything you do? I caught him earlier, pretending that he was smokin' weed and drivin'," she told him.

"Okay, baby, I'll see to him," Javoo said back to her as he continued to position the bills in his safe.

* * *

"WHAT!" was the answer Cornelius got when Shalon answered her phone. She was highly upset at the both of them, and more nervous than anything as Cornelius started to laugh.

"Are you laughing, Nigga? That shit was not funny!" she said, breathing heavily over the phone.

"I'm just callin' to see if you made it ok," he said to her.

"Where's Javoo? At home with his wife?" she asked him in a mean and sarcastic fashion. Cornelius explained to her why Javoo had him to call her. He told her that Javoo wanted her to stay put until he called or came by. But then she told him that Mitchell had been calling her back to back all evening, and that she had not answered the phone. He could sense that she was scared and he did his best to get her to try to stay cool. They had known each other from day one, when Javoo first met her at a sports bar, so she was more than comfortable talking to him, plus he always did joke and joog at her.

"You was crying and everything. I thought you was gon' pee on yourself," he said meddling her. "Fuck you, Nigga! I ain't never done no shit like that before," she said shy-like.

"Well, you know you are officially in now. You might have to quit your day job," he said and then began to laugh again. They continued to talk for a few more minutes. Shalon had seemed to be feeling a little bit better, especially after Cornelius had told her how they knew what they were doing. He made sure she understood what she had done and told her not to worry about Mitchell. Once he realized that she was ok, he hung up the phone and went to go take care of his business with his part of his come-up.

Cornelius lived alone and looked similar to Nelly when you saw him. He drove a pearl-colored Escalade, with Asanti accessories and a chrome set of 24" inch Asanti rims on it. He'd had it customized on the inside, redecorating the interior with crocodile skin and had a massive set of Rockford Fosgate 15" inch speakers mounted in the back. He probably had around $350,000 of his own money stashed out at his mom's house, who now lived in the Hiram Clark area. He mostly spent the night at a different female's house every night, and only came to his own apartment to shower and to change clothes, or to count his money. He'd only allowed Javoo to have a key to his apartment, which was something he couldn't argue at all. How could he refuse that to such a down to earth guy, who had helped him get on his feet over night?

When he and Javoo first met, he was wild and rebellious. He always packed a gun and had somewhat of an itchy trigger finger, as he ran the streets of 3rd Ward with his boy, Deno.

They had been best friends all their lives. They terrorized boys when they got out of line and had been running with the rowdiest clique in the Trey, until Javoo told him that they were hanging with the wrong crowd. He later bumped into Javoo, who was needing someone to help him hit a nice lick, and Cornelius just so happened to be in the right place, at the right time. The rest was history and they had become very close as time passed.

* * *

Shalon quickly answered as soon as she saw Javoo's number pop up on her phone. She wanted to talk to him and was glad that he called when he did.

"Where are you?" she asked once she picked up.

"I'm about to pull up outside," Javoo told her.

"Okay," she said, hung up and then went and unlocked the door for him to come in. As soon as Javoo walked in the door, she ran up to him and hit him in the chest with the side of her fist.

"I'm not doin' no shit like that no more!" she said as he strongly grabbed her and squeezed her tightly.

"I know you mad, Baby, but you did good. You did real good," he said as he whispered down and nibbled on her earlobe. He handed her a purple Crown Royal bag with a big lump inside it.

"Here, I got something for you," he said. Shalon felt on the bag trying to figure out what was in it. He had never given her any presents before and certainly didn't expect what she was about to see.

"What's this?" she asked as she opened the bag to see the money inside.

"It's just a lil somethin' for doin' what you did," he told her. "How much is it?" the gloomy-eyed Shalon asked. "It's 25, 000," he said, then walked to her bedroom to check the place for any other people.

"Why you always do that? Always lookin' around. You know I'm not gon' have nobody up in here but you," she said to him.

"You better not," Javoo said and then laid back on her bed.

Shalon ran and jumped on top of him with the bag of money still in her hand. They kissed as he softly began to rub her back with his hands. Shalon sighed. She had been wearing a large Iceberg T-shirt with a huge picture of Goofy on the front and a pair of panties as she sat up on him allowing his hands to go under her shirt and to her breasts.

"I want you," she said as she criss-crossed her arms and pulled her shirt up and over her head. Javoo rolled her over onto her back and began to kiss her in pecks down the center of her stomach. It felt good to have a side piece as sexy as Shalon and he wanted to make the best of it, so he slowly pulled at her panties as he kissed her waistline. She rose to help them off. Her dark skin was smooth and shined like silk in the darkness of the room.

Quickly, he unbuckled his pants while she pulled his shirt over his head and tossed it on the floor. He kicked off his shoes, then his pants and, with no hesitation, she helped him guide his dick inside her. Another sigh came from her lips as her eyes closed. Slowly, back and forth he moved to the gestures of Shalon.

"I love you, Javoo," she said, as his big black dick, hard as a jawbreaker, throbbed inside her. His repetitions began to speed up as he threw one of her legs up and over his shoulder, then the other. He had positioned her in 10 minutes to two fuck styles that allowed him to go deeper and deeper inside her, as if he were drilling for oil. Shalon's bottom lip was tucked into her mouth and her eyes had become enormously tight, as he continued to pound her like never before.

"Ooooh! You gon' make me cum," she blurted out as she squeezed him tightly. Javoo pulled out and turn her over onto her stomach. He liked fucking Shalon from behind, and it showed once he slipped his dick back inside her again. The arch in her back made him stroke her viciously, as he pressed her head down on the bed with one hand and spread her butt cheeks open with the other. ·

"Whose pussy is this?" he asked as he fucked her from behind.

"It's yo' pussy, uh!" Shalon said, arching her back more and more with every stroke. Javoo began to cum and then collapsed down on top of her.

"Ah, don't move," she said enjoying the climax as he filled her completely inside. They both laid there naked on the bed, comforting each other like two love birds in a nest. To Shalon, it felt like heaven.

* * *

Mitchell stuck his key in the lock and opened the door, thinking to himself how embarrassing it was going to be once he told his girl Tracy that he had been robbed. It was hard for a guy who thought he was all that, to have to say this to a person who thought he was the world. He had been constantly thinking about Shalon and didn't want Tracy to know that he was trying to fuck her friend.

"Hi, baby" Tracy said as soon as he walked into her apartment.

"Hey," he said as she held up her head for a smack on the lips.

"What's wrong?" she asked, sensing that something seemed different about his swagger.

"Something bad happened to me today," he said, reaching into her refrigerator to grab one of her Bartles & James wine coolers.

"Two dudes ran up in my condo and took all of my money," he said, feeling bad about having to even say that. Mitchell was the type that made a woman feel like he was everything and that he was quite untouchable to almost anybody, especially to the goons that lurked the streets of H-Town.

"Oh, my baby-boo," she said as she went over and hugged him. "Are you ok?"

"Yeah, I'm ok," he said and then took another swallow of the wine cooler.

"Well, good thing you listened to me and let me start putting some of your money in the bank for you," she said.

33

"That's what I got you for, right, baby?" he said back to her. "How much do I got in there anyway?" he quickly asked.

"You should have a couple hundred thousand," said Tracy.

Mitchell went on to give her all the details about the robbery, except for mentioning the fact that Shalon was there. He also told her that he needed her to go to the bank to get the money he needed to payoff Money Black.

"I'll find out exactly how much is in there tomorrow and bring the bank statements to you," she said as he kicked off his shoes and sat back on the couch.

"So, what have you been doin' today?" he asked her as she came over and sat next to him, sipping a wine cooler of her own.

"Tryin' not to get robbed," she said in a joking manner, hoping to cheer him up. She then went on to tell him how she ordered a few things from the internet and that her friend had come over.

"Oh, Shalon stopped by today?" he asked with a surprised look on his face.

"Yeah, she was just in the area and decided to stop by, I guess," said Tracy. Tracy and Shalon had been co-workers at a women's store in the Galleria Mall for a couple of years now. Tracy was the manager and Shalon had not too long ago made assistant manager. They were both off on Sundays and Mitchell thought that it could have been any reason why she had stopped by. He knew he didn't mess around with too many niggas in the streets, so somebody had to say something about what he had in his condo, and he was hoping Tracy didn't let her friend come over and peel her for that kind of information.

He just couldn't put it together, either way. After all, he was the one who gave Shalon the directions to his condo and had invited her over in the first place.

"Bitch just better keep her mouth shut," he mumbled to himself, as that turned out to be his only concern.

Chapter Four

The next morning Tracy had already gotten up and headed to the bank. Mitchell laid dead still in her bed and tucked under the covers as the air conditioning blew cold in Tracy's bedroom. His cell phone had been ringing back-to-back-to-back for the past five minutes and it was starting to get on his nerves. He turned to adjust his eyes to the clock that hung on the wall. It was 9:45am.

"Aaaah!" he yawned and then reached over to the night stand to pick up his phone. He looked on the screen hoping that it was Shalon who had been calling him.

"Damn nigga!" he said as he recognized Money Black's number. "She's gone to get it now," Mitchell said as soon as he answered, still sounding sleepy.

"I didn't call you for that, 'cause I know you gon' take care of that business. I got a move for you, that's if you want to get back some of the money you lost yesterday," Money Black said to him.

Mitchell threw the covers back and sat up butt naked on the bed. "It'll be for tonight, so I'll tell you all about it when you come through today," Money Black said and then hung up.

"Wonder what that nigga is talkin' bout," Mitchell said to himself as he went and stood over the toilet to take a piss. He suddenly heard someone scrambling at the front door, and in came Tracy, with her joyful attitude as usual.

"Mitchy baby," she said in a light tone of voice as he heard the front door open and then quickly close. Tracy locked the door, chain and all, while holding her purse tightly under her arm. Mitchell had already told her what happened to him and she wasn't about to take any chances.

"You up?"

"Yeah, I'm up," he said as he slipped into his boxers. Tracy had a couple of Breakfast Jacks in her hand along with an orange juice. She dug into her purse, pulled out five green and white bank envelopes with $11,000 in each and handed them to Mitchell.

"Here is the bank statement, so you won't think I'm tryin' to getcha," she said as she gave him the piece of paper, the food and the envelopes. Mitchell looked at the bank statement as Tracy quickly tried to fix her bed. He'd had just over $250,000 still in the bank and what a relief it was to have listened to her from the start.

"I gotta go to work," she said as she kissed him on the cheek and then turned and headed back out the front door. Now, all he had to do was take Money Black the cash that he owed him

and see what was up with that move he mentioned on the phone.

* * *

Money Black sat behind the desk in his office at his car and accessories shop. He had a couple of foreign cars, along with his BMW, a candy-blue Escalade and a few motorcycles lined up out front as advertisement for his business. Shiny sets of rims filled the inside of the place, as well as speakers, amps, alarms and many other accessories. He also had a pool table in another room at the back of the small building, where a few of his boys shot dice and were joking and laughing with a couple of females. Ting-a-ling-a-ling! The tiny bells on the door jingled as Mitchell walked in.

"Nigga better had brought me my money," Money Black said to himself and then stood and went to meet him. Mitchell passed him a small backpack that contained the money and then tried to shake his hand, but Money Black just turned and told him to follow him to the back. When they walked into the room where they were shooting dice in, everybody immediately got quiet.

"You ho's go up front," he said and snapped his fingers, causing the girls to quickly scramble out of the room.

Mitchell took a seat in a chair against the wall of the room, as he and the other fellas listened to what Money Black had to say.

"Ok, this is what I got," he said as he pulled out a Black and Mild cigar and fired it up. He continued to tell Mitchell and his boys about a guy named Ralph, whom he had been competing with in the drug business, as well as status on who ran the Northside of Houston. Ralph, like Money Black, was breaded up and had made a name for himself when a big time Columbian was found dead near a small apartment complex

39

that he owned. Many people thought that was how Ralph had come-up, because the word on the streets was that at least 500 kilos of the Columbian's dope was stolen from a U-Haul truck that was parked behind one of the Columbian's stores right after he was killed. That come-up wasn't really what ate at Money Black, though. Ralph was an outsider in his book-not originally from the Northside. He had come and started what he thought was a bullshit ass record company and was starting to get recognized by some major players around the city. Money Black didn't like that. He wanted to take Ralph all the way out the game. He wasn't about to let some chump that's done been robbed and everything else come and steal his shine, and he wanted to make sure Ralph knew damn well who the real street legend of the north was.

* * *

Ralph sat behind the wheel of his Aston Martin as he drove down the beltway, talking thru the speaker phone in his car. On the line was Young Thug, one of his favorite rap artists, and Ralph figured that the guy's skills were going to do him a lot of good. He had just started a record label called G-5 Records, which stood for "fly-high", and he'd finally struck a deal with Colossal Records, a major mainstream company that was sure to put him over the top. He had been doing pretty good as far as business was concerned. He did his best to recruit any and every rapper he could possibly sign, mainly because of the competition in town. The rap game in Houston was starting to warm up and he wanted his company to be right there when the light started to shine. 'That was just how he felt about G-5; besides, it was another way for him to push his drugs and the real reason why his clique had grown so fast.

Ralph also oversaw a few other businesses of his own. He had a bail bonds company, two car lots, a small apartment complex, and a small-time record shop that he'd pretty much handed over to his younger sister. He just knew he had it all figured out. He knew that none of his people wanted for nothin'. If they sold dope, then he would front them whatever they needed, as long as they knew the code--"KEEP YOUR MOUTH SHUT!" If they needed a job, then he would let them work at one of his spots; and, if they went to jail, he would bond them out and then go and pick them up in one of the cars from his car lot. His wife, Donna, she was the one that ran the bail bonds company, while his sister, Chi-Chi, ran the record shop. He had a guy named Smooth to run the studio, and a few other people to run the car lots and the apartment complex. He mostly moved his drugs out of state to places like Nebraska and Iowa, where the price for a kilo of cocaine was extremely high. That made it hard for almost anyone to detect his movements.

The cops - they had tried to keep an eye on him after the death of the Columbian, but just couldn't find any real reason to arrest him for the murder or catch him doing anything wrong on the streets. His parents had been killed in a train crash while visiting some relatives in New Jersey, and he and Chi-Chi were awarded over five million dollars from the settlement. So he had a legitimate excuse for having lots of money and owning the businesses that he did. He had a fairly nice two-story pool home, ranging from around $350,000 to $400,000, just off T.C. Jester, where he and his wife Donna lived. A group of tennis courts sat at the corner of his street, where people in his community were able to play in their spare time. He really liked living in that area.

Ralph reached above his head and pressed the garage door opener as he drove down his street and into his driveway. His wife was still at the bail bonds company, finishing up some paper work on a guy she had just bonded out of jail. He thought about her as he walked in the door and decided to give her a call.

"Hey, honey," Donna said as she answered her phone.

"How is everything going?" he asked her.

"Everything is good here, but I'm about to leave," she said, knowing that he wanted her home with him.

"Ok, see you when you get home," he said and then hung up. Donna turned to the guy she had just bonded. He had been making runs for Ralph for a while now and had gotten pulled over by the police and hauled off to jail the night before.

"Okay, don't forget to make your payments on time," she said as she shook his hand as he left. She then pulled out a group of keys and began to lock the file cabinets. She checked the alarm and then turned off the air conditioning when she heard the cling sound of the front door.

"Yes, how can I help you?" she asked as two guys she had never seen before walked in. "We having trouble tryin' to get at somebody and we was hoping that you could help us," said one of the guys.

"Well, what's his name? Maybe we can spring 'em," she said with assurance.

"His name is Ralph," the guy said and then quickly pointed a gun at her. Donna went into shock and stood there frozen in fear. This was the second time in her life she'd had a gun pointed at her, and both times it was something that was pertaining to her husband.

"What do you want?" she asked as she nervously sat down.

"It ain't what we want; it's what we're gonna get," the other guy said as he shut the blinds to the windows and turned to Donna with a look in his eyes that terrified her.

Chapter Five

Money Black sat next to Mitchell and watched as a couple of girls danced naked on top of the pool table in his shop. He had been waiting on a phone call from one of his boys and couldn't wait to go and meet them whenever they called.

"You like that?" he asked as one of the girls winked her eye at Mitchell.

"Yeah, she's sexy," Mitchell said back to him. Mitchell thought about what he had told him on the phone earlier that morning and it had been bugging him all afternoon to know what he had in mind. He had some business he needed to take care of with another female and was wondering why Money Black was insisting that he stick around for a little while longer.

"So what did you want to talk to me about?" Mitchell asked. Money Black went on to thank him for keepin' it real about the money that he owed him. He never did doubt Mitchell because he had been dealing with him for a while now and Mitchell had made him a lot of money, so he knew he still had to have some kinda bread. He had just been robbed and he figured that he may be interested in getting back some of the money he had lost.

That's when he began to put his work in on him. He told him that he had to first understand error when it came to dealing with one's money. Money Black also stated the fact that Mitchell had been set up by Shalon, and that he had zero tolerance for slip-ups, which made Mitchell frown once again. He just couldn't believe she had something to do with what had happened. But Money Black wanted to build a trust bond between the two of them, and he had just the thing that he wanted him to do. That's when his cell phone began to ring. It was one of his boys calling to let him know that they had Donna.

Money Black and Mitchell went outside and got inside a plain-Jane Lincoln Continental with dark tinted windows. He crunk up the car, put it in reverse and then pulled out onto the street in front of his car and accessories shop.

"You ever shot a gun before?" Money Black asked as he opened the console between them and handed Mitchell a Desert Eagle .45 automatic.

"Nah! Not really. I done had several guns before, but I just turn around and sell 'em," Mitchell said, as if he never had any real reason to use one. They pulled up at an old abandoned building, got out and went inside. There, in the middle of the floor, sat a woman blind-folded

in a chair with her hands tied behind her back. It was Donna.

"Ma'am, can you hear me?" Money Black asked as he rubbed her hair softly.

"Yes, I can hear you," Donna said as she sniffled. He questioned her about her husband Ralph and the type of money he might have stashed at home. He also managed to get their address, which was what he really wanted.

"Are you going to kill me?" she asked as she heard one of the guys say that he knew the area. "No, I'm not going to kill you, if you cooperate. You understand, don't you?" Money Black asked as Donna nodded her head. "Do you ever text your husband?" he asked her. "All the time," she answered .

That gave him a brilliant idea.

"Where her purse at?" he asked as he turned to one of the other two guys. The guy gave him Donna's purse and he took it and poured all the contents out onto the floor. He picked up her cell phone and asked for Ralph's number. A smiled grew on his face at the thought of Ralph seeing his. He just loved it when a plan came together.

Ralph was starting to get irritated. His wife should have made it home a long time ago, he thought, as he spoke to his sister on his home phone. His cell phone sat on the coffee table just across from where he was sitting. He could hear it making a funny noise, indicating that he had a message and picked it up to see who it was.

"I'll call you back later, Chi-Chi," he said to his sister and then hung up. He fumbled with the keypad on his phone, noticing that the message was from Donna.

"Why didn't you just call? You know I'm at the house," Ralph said to himself as the letters on the screen read--HAD A FLAT-BAT LOW-LEFT CHARGER AT OFFICE-AT CAVALCADE AND JENSEN. Ralph didn't waste no time changing and then jumping into his big F-250. He knew that she had road-side service, but once before it took the people a couple of hours before they got there, and Cavalcade and

Jensen wasn't exactly a great place to be stranded at that time of the evening.

He turned off T.C. Jester and sped onto the 610 loop, heading towards 1-45. He had planned on having a nice quiet evening with Donna, since their two daughters were with one of Donna's sisters at a carnival in town. It was a little after 6pm. The sun was behind buildings and trees and the headlights of a few cars had begun to show, as Ralph saw the Cavalcade exit and flipped on his signal to exit the freeway. He turned and headed towards Jensen.

"Where is she?" he said as he spotted Donna's car parked in front of an old abandoned building, but didn't see her.

He didn't see any real reason why she would be in that area, but he noticed that her car did have a flat tire and it needed to be repaired.

"Where are you?" he said as he pulled his truck up behind her Infinity. He got out with his cell phone in his hand, looking for her, hoping to spot her across the street or anywhere.

"Need some help?" a voice from behind him asked. Ralph turned to see two unknown faces pointing guns at him.

"What's this all about?" he asked as one of the guys quickly patted him down. He was hoping that these two fools didn't have anything to do with his wife's tire being flat.

"Where is Donna?" Ralph quickly asked. A sense of nervousness filled his body. Something about this whole scene just didn't seem right.

"Step into the building," one of the gunmen said as he opened the door. The other gunmen shoved Ralph hard in the back, pushing him into the door of the building. They had him outnumbered, plus he didn't have his own gun with him, so he had no other choice but to follow their orders and go with them towards the center of the building, where he saw Donna tied to a chair.

"I'm here, Baby," Ralph said as he ran over to her. Donna was glad to hear his voice, but it saddened her to know that she had told those men everything they wanted to know about her husband. She just thought she was doing the right thing and didn't think that Money Black was going to be as cruel as he was.

"They told me they wouldn't kill me if I cooperated," she said to him. One of the guys grabbed Ralph, while the other punched him twice in the stomach, dropping him to his knees.

"I'll give you whatever you want, just let her go," Ralph said, still coughing from the blows to his mid-section. "Now that's what I wanted to hear," Money Black suddenly said as he and Mitchell finally stepped out of a dark corner.

"Tie him up," he said firmly. He was a cruel and conniving fellow, knowing that kidnapping Ralph's wife first would be the thing to do. That was pretty much how it went for almost any man, because when it came down to it, who knows who would go out on a limb.

"So, how much do you think she's worth?" Money Black asked as Ralph finally recognized him.

"Everything man, just let her go," Ralph pleaded in a sorrowful tone of voice.

"I would do that, but I don't see nothin'. You did say you would give anything, didn't you?" Money Black asked in a sarcastic way. Ralph just looked down at the floor.

49

"You see anything?" he asked one of his boys. "You see anything?" he asked as he turned to Mitchell.

"How much money do you want?" Ralph asked him.

"Nigga, I don't want your money. I want your life! Now what do you got to trade for that?" asked Money Black.

"I got two mill at my house, man. I can take you to go get it if you would just let her go," Ralph said as he began to realize the horror of the situation. Money Black suddenly blurted out his address and the number to his home security alarm system. He let him know that he didn't need him to take him anywhere, and that his reign on the streets of the north was over.

"I run this shit, Nigga! I always did," Money Black said and then kissed Donna on the side of her face. Ralph tried to struggle with the rope that was tied tightly around him. He wished he could do something to stop the man, but he couldn't.

"You stay away from her!" he shouted.

"Whatchu gon' do if I don't?" Money Black started laughing.

"This is between me and you, not her. Don't fuck up and do somethin' you gon' regret," Ralph said to him. Money Black frowned as he looked at Ralph. He thought that he had to be out of his mind, talking to him like he was in the position to call some kinda shot.

"Fuck up! Nigga, you fucked up when you didn't come to me and ask for permission to even live on this fuckin' side of town. You and your little record company. You think you can just roll in and do what the fuck you want around here? Nigga, you must be crazy," Money Black said as he handed Mitchell the Desert Eagle.

Mitchell looked at Money Black as he held the big gun in his hand. He didn't know these people and he certainly didn't think that this was gon' be part of Money Black's plan. He knew he wanted him to do something, but he just didn't think it was gon' be somethin' like this.

"Whatchu lookin' at me for, nigga? This yo' chance to prove yourself. Remember the money you just lost," Money Black said as he looked at him. Mitchell walked up to Ralph and put the gun to his head. He didn't want to kill him, but what choice did he have?

"BUST NIGGA!" Money Black said and that's when Mitchell blew Ralph's brains out and then turned and put two shots in Donna's chest as well.

He stood there breathing heavily, with much adrenaline flowing through his veins. His hands trembled as he stood there, still pointing the gun at the lifeless bodies. That's when Money Black walked up to him and took the gun from his hand.

"Good work. I didn't think you had it in you. Now let's get the hell outta here," he said as they all left the building.

Chapter Six

Cornelius stopped at a corner store to get a cup of coffee and some orange mango blunt wraps and watched as a couple of kids wrestled with a few nickels and pennies to pay for candy that they had scattered over the counter before they went to school.

"I got it," he said as he threw a $20 dollar bill on the counter.

"Thank you, mister," the two young children said as they scraped the candy and all the coins off the counter and headed out the door.

"Oh, and let me get one of those Houston Chronicles, too," he told the Iranian store clerk, who was busy punching at the cash register. Cornelius grabbed the items, went out the door and got into his Escalade. He yawned as he fixed the newspaper in his lap, unraveled one of the blunt wraps and then filled it with the orange cush that he and Javoo took from Mitchell's condo. It was early and he had just left the home of a local dancer, who had invited him over for more than just some late night entertainment.

He fired up the engine, put the SUV in reverse, and headed towards his apartment, as he gently puffed on the blunt between his lips. He listened to the Madd Hatta Morning Show and was surprised by what he was hearing. Rappers were calling in to mourn the loss of their CEO at Records, commenting on how much love he showed them, and how the cops seemed to have no leads to finding out who killed the guy and his wife.

"Damn!" he said as he continued to puff on the blunt. He began to think about the time when he had used Ralph's sister Chi-Chi as a way to get into Ralph's home, so that he and Javoo could rob him. It was a lovely come-up but, to him, it seemed that nothing had changed. Ralph was still getting the bad end of the stick, he thought, and then waved back at the female security guard as he pulled into the entrance of his complex and crept slowly to his apartment. He reached into his console, pulled out his .9mm and tucked it into his waist. Then he grabbed the newspaper and the coffee and got out. He couldn't wait to see what the newspaper had to say about the murder, so he quickly unlocked the door to his apartment and went inside.

"Let me see what they talkin' bout," he said as he sat at the table and turned through the paper straight to the section that read: MAN AND WIFE FOUND DEAD IN ABANDONED BUILDING. That's when he picked up the phone and called Javoo's number.

"What's up, Playboy?" Javoo answered. Cornelius could hear the rumbling sound of music playing in the background and then the noisy sound suddenly stopped.

"You heard the news, my nig?" he asked, still puffing on the blunt.

"What news?" Javoo asked him back.

"Remember that boy, Ralph? The one we hit that lick on that time? He and his wife were both murdered last night. It's all over the radio. I'm lookin' at it in the paper right now," said Cornelius.

"You at your spot?" Javoo asked him.

"Yeah, I'm at the crib," he answered.

"I'm about to drop my kids off at school and then I'm gon' come thru," Javoo said and then they hung up. Cornelius sat there and thought about Chi-Chi. He tried to imagine how she must be feeling, but then shook his head, trying to shake off the thought of him knowing how she once felt about him. It had been three years since he'd last saw her, and that was when she and her brother were being duct taped by him and Javoo, which now turned out to be one of his worst memories.

* * *

Mitchell woke up the next morning, feeling way better than the day before. He had gone over to Tracy's with an extra-large duffle bag and a suitcase and when she saw him, she started to smile, because she thought that he was officially moving in. That was until he opened the suitcase and showed her all of the money that was inside it. He had told her that he wanted her to deposit the $55,000 that she withdrew for him and for her to deposit more as the days followed. He made sure he put the $100,000 he needed to hustle with on the streets to the side, and told her not to tell anyone about the money he had hidden in her apartment. He didn't want to get robbed again and he was hoping he could trust her to keep her mouth shut, especially when it came to her friend Shalon.

Mitchell was still a little disorientated by what he had done last night, though. He could hear the Channel 2 news media spokesperson mentioning that the police were still on the scene of the crime, as a quick news flash aired on the TV. That's when he began to think about how he and Money Black had followed the other two guys as they drove over to Ralph's house and found his stash. Money Black had taken 1.1 million dollars, while Mitchell and the other two took $300,000 each and went in their own direction once they left Money Black's car and accessories shop. He never thought that he would have to kill anyone in his life, even though Shalon had made him feel that way just the day before. She still had not answered her phone and now he wasn't even trippin'. What good would it do him to call anyway? He had gotten back way more money than the two haters that invaded his condo had taken from him and now he was thinking that Shalon could just go to hell.

"Bitch-ass-bitch," he said to himself, as if he were actually telling her, "How 'bout that!" when he thought about the robbery. He was back on again, and now he felt that no one was going to stop him.

Chapter Seven

Chi-Chi's eyes were swollen and red from crying all night long. She had received the news of her brother's death and had to go down to the mortuary to identify Ralph's body.

"Why did this happen?" she asked herself as she sat on the couch in her living room, thinking of all the things that she had been through, with her parents being killed when she was much younger, and now her older brother brutally murdered. She felt like she had been left all alone, and with no family. Her brother's two daughters had stayed over to one of Donna's sister's house, who was also trying to get her to stay as well, but Chi-Chi wanted to think things through on her own. Everything she could possibly think of was racing through her head, until her phone suddenly began to ring.

"Hello," she said, not recognizing the number.

"Hi! Is this Ms. Chitora Hastings?" asked the man on the other end of the line.

"Yes, it is," Chi-Chi responded sadly.

"My name is Michael Walsh, of Walsh and Associates Law Firm, and I'm calling you in regards of your brother Ralpheal Hastings," the man said. He continued to speak to Chi-Chi about her brother's insurance policy, the businesses that he owned and all the money that he left her in case anything like this happened.

"I'm going to need you to come in and sign some papers today, Miss," the man said to her.

"Okay, let me get myself together," said Chi-Chi.

"I understand," he said and then gave her the directions to his law firm. Chi-Chi wasn't in the mood to be going out, but this was something that had to be done. She quickly took a shower, got dressed, threw on some eyeliner and lip-stick, grabbed her purse and hit the door. Shortly, she arrived at the Law Firm's building, where Mr. Walsh stood waiting for her. He opened the glass door and directed her to an elevator that led up to his office.

"Right this way," he said as he showed her into his office. He pulled up a chair for Chi-Chi to sit in and then took his own seat behind his desk. He first gave her his condolences and then told her how lucky she was to have a brother like Ralph. It was the least he could do to try to cheer her up. He then explained to her how Ralph had left her a little over five and a half million dollars, and that a check for his two daughters would go to them once a month, until they turn 18, along with 1.5 million each due to his wife being murdered also. That was just the money part of the insurance policy. Ralph had also left her the small record shop, one of his car lots, the small apartment complex and the bail bonds company. The record company itself, G-5 Records, .was left to Smooth, the top producer and president of the company, and the other car lot was left to Mr. Walsh himself.

Chi-Chi couldn't believe that she was in charge of all these things. She wondered how she would be able to run all of the businesses by herself, and then began to remember her brother telling her of each business as he purchased them.

"People will always listen to music," she could hear him say when he bought the record shop.

"People will always need a place to stay," she thought of what he had said about the apartment complex.

"People will always need transportation," she remembered him saying about the car lot.

"People will always go to jail," she could still hear him saying about the bail bonds company, as the lawyer's voice crept slowly back into her ears. He went on to explain to her how Donna's family was accepting the responsibility and custody of the children, as he handed her a pen to sign off the paperwork that he had laid out on the desktop in front of her. "

Can I hire you as my attorney right now, being that you did look out for my brother?" she asked him.

"You sure can," he said as he helped her to her feet and then showed her to the door.

"Your name and number will be in my files as a client, so do call me in any case you need me," the man said as Chi-Chi stepped into the elevator across the hall and then let the doors close to end their conversation.

Chi-Chi was feeling the power her brother once felt, thinking of everything she had just gained. As she drove her yellow Corvette down the freeway, she thought about all the people that might be showing up at her brother's funeral. All of the rappers from G-5, maybe a few of his employees from the businesses she now owned, and even some of his dope dealing buddies. They all were probably going to be there. She also had to stop by Donna's mom's house to consult with them about the funeral arrangements and to see her two nieces.

A soft smile formed on her face as she thought about how they had always looked up to her, wishing that someday they would grow up to be just like her. She even had to call a few relatives out in New Jersey and Chicago, whom Ralph would frequently visit whenever he went their way. She wasted a couple of hours over at her in-laws house, hugged her two nieces and then left, thinking of how life for her was going to be without her beloved brother.

* * *

Javoo and Cornelius sat most of the morning at Cornelius' apartment, smoking weed and throwing who could have killed Ralph up in the air. They finally came up with the thought of the three beautiful girls that they met just yesterday at the Papadeaux Restaurant, and decided to give them a call.

"Well, let's meet up and have lunch," Javoo said, finishing up his conversation with one of the females. Cornelius had already taken a shower and changed for the day. He really wanted to put it down with one of the girls who had been all smiles from the moment they met. He was hoping that she would still be in that same mood as they went outside to where Javoo's car sat next to his Escalade and Cadillac CTS.

"C'mon, ride with me," Javoo said as they went and got inside his Maserati. Javoo was very stylish and knew how to dress and what to drive on any occasion. His flyness was well accepted by almost anyone and his street game was definitely

on another level. That was his gift. He was a street mastermind
and gettin' money was his specialty. They had hit a major lick
when they hit Mitchell, and wasn't nothing really going on, so
they had time to fuck off, as they sped down the 610 freeway
to Meyerland, where they pulled into the parking lot of a steak
house once they exited the freeway.

"They should already be inside," Javoo said as they took
the front steps of the restaurant and went in.

"There they are," Cornelius said and pointed to a girl in a
far corner waving her hand in the air, signaling for them as
they stood at the entrance. They went over to the table and
greeted them with hugs.

"So what's up?" one of the girls asked as they scooted over
to give them room to sit with them.

"We came to check y'all out, you know, to see what the
business is," Cornelius said, rubbing elbows with the girl that
was sitting next to him. A waitress came over to take their
orders as they giggled and laughed throughout the process.
These three girls were like no others you would meet on an
average day. One was a flight attendant, who was on a three-
week vacation and was hanging out with her friends. Another
worked for the U.S. Customs and Transportation Department
out at the Intercontinental Airport, and the third was a high-
priced real estate agent, who had been friends with the other
two for quite some time.

"So how did y'all meet?" Javoo asked them, as they sipped
the drinks the waitress had brought them.

"We used to be strippers, back when Lip Sticks was open," one of the girls said, not feeling ashamed of her past. Javoo and Cornelius quickly looked at each other.

"I knew it was something I liked about y'all!" Cornelius said as the girls all began to smile.

Javoo thought of how lovely this all sounded to him. Their occupations and them being freaks all added up. They had to know some people who knew some people, he thought.

He figured that these girls were truly some mainstream resources, and he was hoping that he could use them in the near future. His root beer-colored Maserati had already spoken for him, as well as his swag and it showed when it came to these three girls. He liked them and he knew that they liked him. Their ethnic backgrounds were exotic starting with Laura, the flight attendant. She was from Barbados. The other one was Marissa. She was from right there in Houston, but originated out of Brazil when she was just 5 years old. The last girl was Stephanie, a war baby. She was a half-black and half-Vietnamese chick whose father was a colonel in the military back in the day. She was a bad bitch.

As their food arrived, they made plans for the weekend. The girls invited Javoo and Cornelius to a party Saturday night, on the roof-top of a loft building that a friend of theirs owned. They both agreed to go. They wanted to see just what kinda people these girls knew, who they kicked it with and what kind of information they could come up on. They even amazed them by leaving a couple hundred dollars as tips for the waitress.

"Oooh! Big tippers. You guys are spoilers," Marissa said as they all turned and walked out of the restaurant. Javoo's car had just so happened to be parked just a few cars over from Stephanie's. She had already been admiring his style and now she was admiring his class.

"Nice ride," she said as the taillights on his Maserati flashed when he hit the alarm key pad.

"Thank you, but it's not as nice as yours," Javoo pointed at her ass and said, as the girls all giggled and waved bye to them.

Chapter Eight

Shalon felt nervous about seeing Tracy at the store where they worked. Her conscience bothered her as she thought about the role she had played to set up Mitchell, and how Javoo and Cornelius had taken all of his money and left. But still, she thought the role he played in front of his own girl-friend and how he had been trying to get at her the whole time was a bad thing for him. She knew he didn't want Tracy to know what he had been trying to do. He had invited her over to his condo true enough; but, the fact was, if she didn't have anything to do with the robbery, then what was she doing there in the first place?

"Hope she doesn't know anything," she said to herself as Tracy smiled when she walked in. She and Tracy were real cool with each other, one always looking out for the other, as their relationship grew. Shalon didn't want to ruin that. She didn't want to mess things up around the job either and she was glad that Tracy had never even seen Javoo before.

"What's up, girl?" Tracy said as she walked into the small room where they kept their purses.

"Nothin' much, what's up with you?" Shalon asked her back, glancing at her as she fixed her nametag on her blouse.

"I think Mitchell is coming to take me to lunch today. You're welcome to come if you want," said Tracy. Shalon really didn't want to see Mitchell again…ever! But as long as she and Tracy worked together, she knew that there was a strong possibility of that happening.

"Nah, you two go ahead. I wouldn't want to crowd y'all," Shalon said, giving Tracy her excuse not to go. "Plus, I have an errand to run," she quickly said to seal the offer shut. She had already planned to go to her bank and deposit some of the money Javoo had given her, as her bank account hardly had any money in it at all. She was a true shopaholic, a free spender, and money didn't last too long in her possession.

Shalon and Tracy both continued to make small talk about a couple of reality shows as customers started to come in and out of the store. "May I help you?" Shalon asked a jazzy looking female who had just walked in.

"Yes, I'm looking for something more on the formal side," said the female.

"Care to speak on the occasion?" Shalon asked, eager to help.

"Well, it's for a wake," the girl said.

"Okay, right this way," Shalon said and then directed her to a rack of very delicate fabrics.

"Hope you find something you like," she said and walked away, seeing that the girl wasn't in the mood for any small talk. Shalon looked at her watch and thought about going to the bank, when she suddenly heard a male voice in the store. It was Mitchell. He had already come to see if Tracy was ready to go on her break.

Tracy was the manager of the store, so she spent a lot of time sitting behind the counter and filling out paper work, as she spoke surprisingly to him.

"Hey there!" she said, standing up to go and get her purse. Mitchell had quickly redirected his eyes over to where Shalon was standing. He gave her the ugliest stare he could find as he stood there and watched her straighten the hangers on a few racks.

"Not speaking today, Shalon?" he asked, just to see how she was going to react. He knew they usually would be joking around, but now that he done been robbed, the atmosphere between them was totally different.

"Excuse me!" the female customer said to Mitchell as he leaned on the counter by the cash register.

"Oh, I'm sorry," he said, jerking himself aside so that the girl could lay her items on the counter. Shalon came over to ring up the things the girl wanted to buy as she shouted out to Tracy, who was still in the back of the store.

"I'll go on break when you get back," she said to get Tracy's attention. She didn't want to go through this. She was ready for her and Mitchell to leave.

"That will be $207," Shalon said to the girl as she put the clothing into a shopping bag. The girl paid for her clothes, grabbed her bag and left the store. So did Tracy and Mitchell.

Chapter Nine

Money Black was feeling like a king as he kicked back in a chair at his car and accessories shop. He knew that a lot of Ralph's customers were going to start coming his way. He even had the audacity to call and try to see if he could purchase G-5 Records as the CEO, but everything about the label had been put on hold due to the murders. He nodded his head and presented a wicked smile. He was overly satisfied by what he had done as he thought about the way that Mitchell was acting after he had pulled the trigger on Ralph and Donna.

"You under my wing now," he said to himself, thinking of how he had Mitchell by the balls. He knew that when it came down to it, he wasn't going to be the one who had actually pulled the trigger and got charged with the initial murder. In his mind, he was going to find some kinda way to put it all off on Mitchell. He also knew that his plan was sinister enough for Mitchell to keep his mouth shut about the murders.

A couple of youngsters came in looking at some amplifiers, and talked to each other as they pointed at a couple of amplifiers and speakers. "Man! I was supposed to finish up my album this weekend, too," one of the youngsters said to the other.

"Yeah, that's messed up what happened to Ralph," the other youngster said as Money Black listened in on their conversation.

"So, what y'all need?" a guy asked as he walked behind the counter of Money Black's shop. One of the youngsters began to speak as he pulled out a wad of money.

"I need somethin' that will push six twelves. The amp I got now is fried," the youngster said to him.

"Six twelves, huh?" the guy said as he started to explain to the youngster about what he really needed.

"You need one amp on two speakers each, so that all six speakers won't drain the amp's power, making it get hot too fast. That's why the amp you got now is fried," the guy told the youngster.

"Y'all hook up music, too?" the youngster asked him.

"Yeah! Our music guy is out back hookin' one up now," the guy said as the youngsters both heard a bumping sound coming through the back wall of the place. The youngster paid for three amps, a set of six-by-nines, a couple of tweeters and then went outside to move his car around back.

Money Black sat there wondering if the youngsters worked on the streets for Ralph. He then thought about the record company and how much that studio and all would help his pockets.

"And I wouldn't even change the name," he said as he got up and walked to the back of the building where the youngsters were.

"So, what do they call y'all?" Money Black asked as he came out and walked over to where they were standing.

70

"They call me Young Thug and that's my boy Creepy," the youngster said. Money Black continued to question them about who they thought would take charge of the label. The youngsters told him that Smooth, the label's top producer, was the only one in charge and that all they knew was that Ralph's sister had come in to talk to him.

"Smooth and Ralph's sister, huh!" Money Black said as he turned and walked back inside the building. He had to find a way to get that record label. But first, he had to find out who was really in charge of it and he knew just who he could get to find out.

* * *

A few days later ... The church that was holding the wake for Ralph and Donna's bodies was over-crowded with people from everywhere and every walk of life. Chi-Chi looked around as people chattered in small groups, some viewing the bodies and so forth.

"I don't even know most of these people," she said to one of Donna's sisters. Donna's mom was sitting near Chi-Chi and she could hear her start to cry every time someone placed flowers next to Donna's coffin.

"Chitora!" an elderly woman said as she walked up to Chi-Chi. It was her aunt from New Jersey.

"Aunt Gladys, I'm so glad you made it," she said as she stood to hug her.

"Oh baby, I'm sorry that this happened. Are you doing ok?" her aunt asked as she rubbed her hands.

71

"Yes ma'am, I'm fine," Chi-Chi replied and then began to introduce her to Donna's family. They squeezed her in on the crowded front bench and that's when the woman went on to tell Chi-Chi that if she needed anything, she knew that she could always come to her, and how Ralph had always been one of her favorite nephews. They continued to talk socially with Donna's family and all took turns comforting Ralph and Donna's two daughters, who were sitting on the bench next to them.

The night seemed to drag on for Chi-Chi, as the people inside the church started to thin. Chi-Chi's aunt had already left for her hotel, which was another thing that bothered her just a little. She had offered to let her stay at her house, but the woman insisted on staying at the hotel.

"Ok, see you at the funeral, girl," one of Donna's sisters said as they hugged and shedded a few more tears together.

"Excuse me, um Chi-Chi!" a guy said as Chi-Chi turned to acknowledge him.

"Hi," she said to the guy, noticing that he was dressed in a three-piece suit.

"You don't know me, but I was a good friend of your brother's. We used to go out of town together on business," the guy said as they stepped aside to let a couple pass.

"Ok, and you are?" Chi-Chi asked.

"My name is Anthony. Everybody calls me Tony," he said.

"I think I might have heard my brother mention that name before," she said.

"Well, I have something to share with you, if you have the time," Tony said. He went on to tell Chi-Chi how he had made a run for Ralph one night, got pulled over by the cops and was hauled off to jail.

"Your sister-in-law, Donna, came to bond me out, and as I was leaving I remembered seeing two guys pulling up at the bail bonds company in a candy blue Escalade," he said, sounding genuinely concerned.

"I don't know if it means anything to you, but that blue Escalade belongs to a guy that works for Money Black," he told her. He went on to tell her how Money Black so called "ran" a certain part of the Northside, and that he hated Ralph because everybody was tryin' to be down with him and what he was doin' with G-5 Records.

"I just thought you should know that," Tony said, shook her hand, and then walked away. Chi-Chi was quite confused about the information the guy had just given her.

"Money Black! What does he have to do with what happened to my brother?" she asked herself as she walked to her car. She didn't even know who Money Black was. She knew that Ralph had money, and that he did his business in the streets, but she also knew that he didn't have to deal with certain people. Still, it all felt strange how Tony came to her like he did, and now she was starting to wonder if Money Black was the one who killed her brother.

Driving down the freeway, Chi-Chi turned up the volume on her radio. Her yellow Corvette dipped from lane to lane as she sped towards her side of town and then turned on her street. As she pulled into her driveway, she could hear the strong sound of the car's engine as the garage door opened.

"Finally made it home," she said as she parked the car and stepped out. She had been gone all day, having to run all kinds of errands and to meet and talk with people about business. She looked and noticed a car with dark tinted windows pulling up in front of her home.

A guy stepped out and approached her as she stood next to her car in the garage. She didn't know what to expect, being that she was Ralph's sister and that he knew so many people.

"Hello, how are you?" the guy asked.

"I'm doing ok," she said as the guy introduced himself.

"My name is Mitchell," he said. Mitchell felt kinda funny talking to Chi-Chi, especially since he was the one who killed her brother. He just figured there was no way she was supposed to know he had something to do with it.

"Yeah, you look familiar. I think I saw you somewhere before," Chi-Chi said to him.

"You know what? Now that you mentioned it, I think I saw you somewhere before, too," said Mitchell.

"The mall! Yeah, you came to pick up your girlfriend, I think," she said.

"Well, I was wondering if you were going to be running the studio for your brother?" he asked. He thought that maybe she was going to tell him that she was gon' be the sole owner of the label, but she told him that her brother didn't leave the company to her, and that he had left it to his good friend Smooth.

"Do you know if the label will be shut down, or if the guy would want to sell it? If so, I might be interested in buying it,"

Mitchell said as if he was actually going to be the one to purchase it.

"I doubt it," she said, tucking her purse tightly under her arm to shut her car door. "Ok then, Miss, I'm sorry to bother you," Mitchell said and then walked back to his car and left.

"Did he follow me?" Chi-Chi asked herself as she went inside and locked all the doors and windows to her place. It was a coincidence how a guy had come to her at the wake and told her about some guy named Money Black, and now all of a sudden another guy showed up at her home, already trying to buy Ralph's record label.

"This doesn't make any sense," she said, digging a small .25 automatic handgun out of a shoebox in her closet and placing it under her pillow. She had to have some answers and soon. The cops still had not found any leads to the people who had murdered her brother, and something was telling her that they never would. She was left with only one solution, as far as getting some help was concerned, and tomorrow she was going to take a shot at it.

Chapter Ten

Money Black's phone began to ring as he sat in the VIP section of his favorite strip club. He had been going to Harlem Knights for years and was an all-time regular to the owner of club. He would let his girls flock around him and a few more fellas as long as they wanted, and if he didn't pay for his drinks that night, he would just put it on his tab for the next time that he came.

"Hello!" he shouted, as he answered his phone and turned his head to the side to adjust to the loud music that was playing in the club.

"I caught up with her," Mitchell said to him about Chi-Chi. Money Black waved the half-naked girl out of his lap and went and stood in a dark corner to talk to him.

"What did she say?" he asked him. Mitchell told him that Ralph's sister didn't own the record company and that it had been left to a guy named Smooth, one of her brother's good friends. Money Black nodded his head continuously. He and Smooth had grown up together in the same neighborhood, so he knew what kinda dude Smooth really was. He had started out as a dope peddling flunky for him, but when Ralph started the record company he jumped ship and got on his band-wagon. He had quickly went from being manager to president of the company, and now it appeared that he was the owner.

THE OWNER! Money Black didn't like that shit- not one bit. He didn't like the fact that when he and Javoo got into it one night at a club out on the Southside, Smooth just stood aside and did nothin' when Javoo knocked him on his ass. That was a few years ago, and ever since then he had always thought of Smooth as scary and looked at him as a ho'-ass nigga.

"Okay, good work "Money Black said to Mitchell and then hung up the phone. He sat back in the chair as the stripper, now fully naked, except for ten-inch transparent high heels, came back over to give him a lap dance of her own.

"Any time you want it, it's yours," the talented girl said as she rubbed herself up and down Money Black's chest in one smooth motion. But he now had Smooth on his mind. He knew everything about the man. He knew where he lived, where his mother lived, the neighborhood he was from and who he hung with. Smooth wasn't hard to find at all, and Money Black would soon go to visit his old friend.

* * *

Cornelius and a female friend had been at the mall shopping after he'd spent half of the morning at a detail shop getting his ride cleaned up. He had planned to meet up with Javoo later that evening for the party that they had been invited to a few days ago.

"So, are you coming over tonight or what?" the girl asked him as he walked her to her car.

"Maybe. I don't know yet. I got somethin' up for this even-ing," he said as she crossed her arms and watched as he opened her door.

"But you said you was," she smacked her lips and said.

"I'll just call you, ok?" he said as the girl got into her car and crunk it up.

"Ooooh, you make me sick," she said, seeing Cornelius smile devilishly as he closed her door. He walked to his Escalade, hit the alarm, opened the back door and put his bags in. He then pulled out a fresh pair of Prada sunshades that he had just bought, put them on and got in.

"I wonder what my boy Deno is up to?" he asked himself, thinking of his old neighborhood homey, as he backed out and left the parking lot.

It had been a while since Cornelius had last drove through his old neighborhood. His mom had moved out to Hiram Clark a few years back, but they had lived in the trey ever since he was a baby boy. She just couldn't take what was going on in the hood anymore. It had become drug infested many years ago, which was one of the main reasons she had wanted to move. He could still remember the time when someone had broken into their house, while they were asleep, and his mom screamed to scare off the burglar. As time passed, he'd ended up being one of the ones who terrorized the hood, he and his boy Deno, and now he was about to see if anything about the hood had changed at all.

His Escalade rumbled as he exited the 288 freeway and turned onto Elgin Street.

"The block still looks the same," he said, turning left at the light on Dowling and then made a right on McGowen Street. He pulled up to a house where a candy-red convertible sat in the driveway and blew the horn. The door to the house quickly opened and that's when Deno stepped out.

"What 's up, boy?" Cornelius asked as he got out. They embraced and then got back inside the Escalade to talk and smoke one for the good old times.

"Say, man! This chick came through here lookin' for you today," Deno said to him.

"Oh yeah?" Cornelius said, still puffing on the blunt.

"Yeah, she was in a yellow Corvette," said Deno.

"A yellow Corvette?" Cornelius said, trying to figure out who it could've been.

"Yeah. You remember those two jazzy-lookin' chicks we met at Herman Park that time? I think she ended up bein' yo' gal," Deno said jokingly.

"What did she look like?" Cornelius asked, still trying to remember who he was talking about.

"She looked real good, my nig. Looked like she had been to church or somethin'. She was dressed all up," Deno said and then started to choke from the blunt they were smokin'.

"She asked me if I had seen you around lately. She gave me this number and told me to tell you to call her," Deno said as he dug the number out of his pocket.

Cornelius looked at the number, picked up his cell phone and pushed in the numbers.

"Hello?" a girl answered with a little bit of excitement in her voice.

"Somebody leave a message for Cornelius?" he asked.

"Hey Cornelius, this is Chi-Chi," she said, causing him to go silent over the line. His eyes grew big. He had not seen her in over three years, and the last thing he could think of was when he and Javoo had robbed her brother.

"So, what's up?" he cautiously asked.

"I need to talk to you," she told him. Cornelius had just remembered seeing the murder of her brother in the newspaper. He had hoped that she wasn't trying to be slick and have him arrested, thinking that he and Javoo might of had something to do with Ralph's murder.

"You need to talk to me about what?" he asked her.

"It's not whatchu think, man. Can you please meet me somewhere so we can talk?" she asked him. "It's real important," she quickly added.

Cornelius thought for a second. He knew he wasn't the one who killed her brother, and he really wasn't worried about that stunt he and Javoo had pulled back when.

"Where do you want to meet?" he asked her.

"Can you meet me over by the Southside Smoke Shop, off 1-45 in about 30 minutes?" she asked him.

"Yeah, I guess I can," he said.

"Okay, bye," Chi-Chi said and then hung up.

Cornelius talked to Deno for a few more minutes, telling him everything that was going on with Chi-Chi and then he left. He knew that he was taking a chance going to see her. What if she really had the cops waiting on him, he thought? But still, there was something that just told him to go and see her.

He sped down the 1-45 freeway from 3rd Ward towards the Smoke Shop. He knew that Chi-Chi didn't know what kind of ride he was gon' be in and he wanted to get there ahead of her so that he could do his own surveillance by parking at the store across the street.

He had been sitting there for about 10 minutes, when suddenly he saw a yellow Corvette speed by and turn into the parking lot of the Smoke Shop. It was Chi-Chi. He quickly looked around to see if anyone was following her, but was distracted by the sound of his phone and looked to see that she was calling him.

"I'm here," she said as soon as he answered his phone.

"Okay, I see you," he said as he pulled out of the store's parking lot and drove over to where she was parked. He pulled up on her driver's side and quickly got out. When Chi-Chi saw him and what he was riding in, she jumped out and ran to hug him. At first she seemed so excited about seeing him, but then her smiling face turned to tears.

"What's wrong?" he asked, feeling sorry for her. Chi-Chi was still crying.

"C'mon and get in," he said as he guided her to the passenger side of his Escalade and helped her in. He turned and began to walk to his side of his ride, thinking to himself how fine and sexy Chi-Chi was to him. When he got in she had started to dry her eyes and then she told him how her brother had left her all the businesses and all the money, which was a plus in his book. The thought of her being his girl again instantly flashed in his head, as she went on to tell him how a guy at her brother's wake told her something about a guy named Money Black.

"A guy even came by my house, because he thought that I was going to take over my brother's record company," she said sounding sad.

"A guy came by your house? Did you know him?" Cornelius asked her.

"No, I didn't know him, but he wanted to know if my brother's label and studio was gon' be for sale. He said his name was Mitchell," Chi-Chi said as Cornelius looked at her.

It couldn't have been the same Mitchell that he and Javoo had just recently robbed. He knew that the guy didn't have the kind of money to purchase a record label that was starting to make some noise. But still, it was surprising enough to him, because he knew that Mitchell got his dope from Money Black and that was enough to keep him listening.

Chi-Chi began to tell him how the police still didn't have any leads to her brother's murder and that the guy at the wake said that he saw two of Money Black's people going to the bail bonding company in a candy-blue Cadillac Escalade as he was leaving. Now everything was starting to add up to Cornelius, but he still wondered what she wanted with him.

He had always felt like she would never speak to him again, especially after what he and Javoo had done to her brother in the past.

"So why did you come looking for me?" Cornelius asked her.

"I didn't know anybody else I could go to besides you," she told him.

"Why didn't you go to the police and tell them what you told me?" he asked.

"You have all this money, you could have posted a reward for the killers," he said, now sounding sincere.

"Cornelius, the cops don't care about my brother. It's like they ain't even tryin' to find out who killed him. They keep tellin' me and my sister-in-law's family that they are looking into it, but they ain't done nothin'. I know that you are always on the streets. Man, I ain't never seen nobody do what y'all did that time and that's why I came looking for you," she said as tears began to flow from her eyes once more. Cornelius slid down in his seat and put his hands on his head. The girl was in distress and refusing her right to her face would do nothing but hurt her even more.

"Could you please check it out for me? I'll pay you or whoever, if you could find the person that killed my brother," she said as Cornelius looked at her.

"Look, you don't have to do that, Baby,'" he said.

"Cornelius, I'm serious. I'll pay you a million dollars if you help me," she said in almost a beggar's tone. Cornelius took another look at her. He could see that she was for real.

"Okay, okay!" he said sounding frustrated.

"You go home, ok, and watch yourself. I gotta make a phone call and then I'll call you later," he said, almost agreeing to help her. Chi-Chi kissed him on the cheek and then got out. She got back in her car, backed out and drove away. Cornelius watched her leave. He couldn't believe that he had just had that conversation with her. She had just offered him a whole lot of money, but to him it wasn't even about that. It was about the way she made him feel and now he had to do more than just help her, he had to make up with her as well.

Chapter Eleven

Javoo had been spending all day with Tanasia and the kids. They had gone to the Kemah Fun Park and Seafood Restaurant, where they rode the roller coaster rides, went out on the boats and after, they had eaten the seafood buffet. Everyone felt tired and drained for the day, as they pulled into their driveway. His son Javon was asleep in the back seat of his Range Rover and his daughter Natasia was nearly asleep as well.

"Come on, Kid," he said, picking up his son and laying him to his chest while Tanasia got their daughter out on the other side. He looked at Tanasia and knew that she was going to have an attitude once he told her that he was going to leave for the rest of the evening. That was mainly because they had had such a lovely day together. But she knew him and she knew him well. It was Saturday night and she knew that he wanted to make his rounds. She knew that he could never sit still a whole day, especially on the weekend.

He laid his son in bed and then went into his own bedroom to turn on the shower. He was going to go to the party that the three lovely women had invited him and Cornelius to. He was just the type to recognize an opportunity, and he wasn't going to pass that up.

"Your phone is ringing," Tanasia said as she watched the screen on his cell phone light up. Javoo stepped out of his closet and answered it.

"What's up?"! he said, recognizing Cornelius's number.

"I got something that I seriously need to holla atcha about," Cornelius told him.

"Oh yeah, what about?" he asked.

"We got a job offer," Cornelius said, now finally feeling like the man in charge.

"Ok, we'll talk about it tonight," Javoo said as Tanasia listened in on their conversation.

"Cool!" Cornelius said and then hung up. Javoo turned to Tanasia as she laid across the bed.

"Come take a shower with me," he said, as Tanasia sluggishly pulled herself away from the bed, unbuttoned her bra strap and got out of her clothes. She got into the shower with him. He held her close and began to tell her that he was going out and that he may be coming in late.

"I got some business to take care of, baby, so try not to give me a hard time, ok?" he said to her in a smooth manner.

"But why can't you take care of that business tomorrow?" she asked him. Javoo looked at her, knowing that she wanted him to stay at home with her.

"Baby, this is something that I gotta do," he said as they washed each other and then got out of the shower. Javoo had a white Mercedes S600 parked in his garage that he had hardly driven. He usually would keep it locked in a storage building, along with his Maserati, but he had gone the night before and pulled it out, leaving his Impala parked there instead.

"I guess I'll hurt 'em with the Benz tonight," he said as he crunk up the car, remembering the girls seeing him in his Maserati. He picked up his phone and called Cornelius as he pulled out of his driveway.

"I'm comin' by now," he said once Cornelius answered. After Cornelius hung up, Javoo wondered what job he was talking about. He had always been the one to come up with the scams, the moves they always made, and now his young homey was starting to do the same, he thought. He knew Cornelius had grown to be a much smarter street thug than the young silly Cornelius used to be, and Javoo wanted to know just what was on his mind.

"Now, what's the deal?" Javoo asked Cornelius once he walked into his apartment. Cornelius started to tell him about everything that went on that day.

"Man, the world sure does work in mysterious ways. Guess who I talked to today?" Cornelius asked him.

"C'mon and spit it out, nigga," Javoo said as he picked up a blunt that Cornelius had sitting in an ash-tray and fired it up.

"I talked to Chi-Chi," he said.

Javoo gave him a surprised look.

"You talkin' about the chick you used to date and the same chick whose brother just got smoked, right?" Javoo asked him.

"Yeah, yeah!" Cornelius said, cutting him off. He went on to tell him how she had went through 3rd Ward looking for him and bumped into his homey Deno, whom she had left her phone number with, so that he could contact her.

"So you went on and took the chance of callin' her huh?" Javoo asked him.

"Well, I really didn't know who the number belonged to at first, so I called just to see. When she came over the line, I did get a little nervous, but she didn't sound like she was up to anything. Plus, I knew that move we made on her brother happened a while back, and I just figured she wasn't trippin' on that no more," Cornelius told him.

"So what happened?" asked Javoo.

"She met up with me and told me somethin' about some nigga comin' to her about Money Black," Cornelius said.

"Money Black!" Javoo said with another surprised look.

"Yeah, she thinks he might have somethin' to do with her brother gettin' killed, and that the nigga said he saw some of Money Black's people at the bail bonding company, where her brother's wife worked," Cornelius said, giving Javoo the whole story.

"So what's up with that job you was talkin' about?" Javoo asked him.

"Well, I know how much you like money, 'cause you know I like money too. She wants to hire us to find out if Money Black killed her brother," Cornelius said as Javoo smiled like he had just heard a joke.

"Whatchu smilin' at, my nig?" he asked.

"Hire us! Get off the gas," Javoo said and then hit the blunt again. "She say she'll pay us a million dollars," he quickly said, causing the smile on Javoo's face to instantly disappear.

"How does she figure that we can find that out? Money Black lives on a completely different side of town," Javoo said to him. Cornelius went on to tell him how Chi-Chi felt that they were pro's on the streets. He knew that if he told Javoo about the million dollar offer, then maybe he would want to check it out.

Javoo sat there for a second trying to gather his thoughts on the whole thing. Her offering them a million dollars was music to his ears and he wanted to hear a little more.

"Did she say anything else? Any details?" Javoo asked, already sounding like a private investigator.

"She said the dudes that went to the bail bonding company were in a candy-blue Cadillac Escalade, and guess what else? She said that nigga Mitchell even showed up at her crib, asking her about her brother's record company," Cornelius said, now getting Javoo's full attention. Javoo knew that Mitchell scored his drugs from Money Black. It was like a small puzzle to him.

"Well, let me think about it," he said, sounding like he was going to roll with it. They gathered up their car keys and cell phones and left for the party.

* * *

Smooth sat at a stoplight waiting for the light to change. He had also gone to Ralph's funeral earlier that day and was on his way home, after seeing a female friend of his. He drove a nice looking stainless steel colored Porsche on a daily basis and would always have it parked in front of G-5 Records whenever he was busy up at the studio. He and his old girl-friend had just recently split up, after she caught him having sex with another girl in the back of the studio. So now, he was single and was lovin' it.

He had been renting a nice looking home, just off of FM 1960, from a couple who was moving to Atlanta and wanted someone that was going to take care of the house to live in it. He felt tired as he pulled into his driveway, for he had been gone the entire day.

"Man!" he said as he thought about his boy Ralph. He began to think about how he was going to fulfill Ralph's dreams in the music business, as he thought about the conversation he'd had with Colossal Records earlier that week. He'd assured them that he could complete the $20 million dollar deal Ralph had struck with them, and had finally came to an agreement on a later date, for the release of Young Thug's album, since Ralph had been killed and he had taken over as the new CEO of G-5 Records. He also thought about the attorney that had him to sign off as sole owner of G-5 Records. He seemed to be a pretty good dude, especially since he'd told him that he was going to represent Ralph's sister Chi-Chi and that he would be available in any case that he needed him as well.

Smooth wrestled with his keys as he unlocked his door and went in.

"Chaaaamp! Here Champ," he said and then whistled for his 6 month old Rottweiler, who would usually come jumping all over him whenever he came in. But on this particular night, he was nowhere to be found.

"Damn dog!" he said after getting no response. He reached over to flip on the light switch and was stunned when he heard a voice coming from the back of his living room.

"Smooth-Smooth-Smooth!" Money Black said as he sat on Smooth's couch with two guys standing next to him.

"Whatchu doin' in my house?" Smooth asked angrily.

"Whatchu do with my dog?" he quickly asked as Money Black began to speak.

"That mutt is ok. We locked him in the bathroom," Money Black calmly said.

"Whatchu want, Nigga?" asked Smooth.

"I just came to talk a little business," said Money Black.

"You broke in my house just to talk? Nigga, you could've just called," Smooth said back to him. Money Black was already tired of hearing Smooth's mouth.

"Shut this fool up!" he said as the other two guys grabbed Smooth and held him. "So you're the owner of G-5 Records, huh?" he said, getting no reaction from Smooth.

"I want that label," Money Black told him. Smooth looked at him like he had to be crazy. He knew he didn't know nothing about producing no music and he was thinking that Money Black had to be out of his mind. He told him that the label had just merged with a mainstream record company and that he had a $20 million dollar deal that the label had to fulfill. He also told him that he was responsible for producing the music of several artists and didn't have time to be foolin' around with some neighborhood homey who didn't know a thing about the music business. He did his best to let Money Black know that he was no way in hell, about to sell that company, but Money Black was thinking different.

"I bet we can make that happen, but after you sell me the business," Money Black said as he stood up and walked over to him.

He told him that he would keep him as president of the company, and so he would still get paid the same as he did when Ralph was alive.

"I'll even give you a whole mill for the label," Money Black said to him. He still had the money he had stolen from Ralph's house, so it wouldn't have hurt him at all to purchase the label, as long as Smooth would go along with the whole thing.

"Do we have a deal or what?" Money Black asked him, as if there was another choice.

"I-I-I can't sell the label," Smooth stuttered and said. Money Black turned and walked over to the couch where he had a gas can sitting on the floor. He picked up the container, untwisted the top, and started pouring gas all over his furniture, and then came over and started to pour gas all over him as well.

"Damn man! Whatchu doin'?" Smooth asked, spitting gas out of his mouth.

"Do we have a deal?" Money Black asked as he took a Black and Mild cigar out of his pocket and lit it up. Smooth knew that he would burn him alive. He had seen him do some awful things to people, even as a kid.

"C'mon man! Don't do this," Smooth said as he watched the cherry on the end of the cigar light up when Money Black pulled on it.

Money Black wasn't in the mood for any games.

He began to tell Smooth how he wished he would've stayed down with him and his younger brother C-Dub, and how he tripped out on him a few years back when he just stood there lookin' like a dummy, when he got into it with that nigga in the club.

"Nigga, I'll burn yo' ass up. You know I don't play," Money Black said as he took the cigar out of his mouth and made like he was gon ' drop it in the small puddle of gas Smooth was standing in.

"Ok, ok!" Smooth said nervously.

"Ok, I'll do it, " he said again quickly. Money Black told him how he would have someone watching him and that he better not go to the police. He then had him to make a call to the attorney that had him sign off as sole owner of G-5 Records and then to Colossal Records about the change in ownership of the label. Now, all they had to do was meet with the attorney and go over the paperwork.

* * *

The party was just as Javoo thought it would be. All kinds of upiddy people were talking and socializing. It looked like a Hollywood scene. There were doctors and lawyers, corporate people, and then there were small business owners, a few Houston Texans football players and Rockets players. There were even musicians, computer heads, models and even movie production people. A man with a camera was walking around taking photos of everyone.

To Cornelius, it was like a Star Magazine shoot. Javoo and Cornelius both stood out like a sore thumb, as a guy walked up to them and spoke. "Hello Sir, .and who do you represent?" the man asked, as he handed Javoo a drink.

"I represent the children of the city. My wife and I own one of the largest daycares around. You might have heard of it. It's called Best Wishes Children's Center and this is a friend of mine," Javoo said before the man could turn to Cornelius.

Javoo knew how to act professional and he knew how to carry a professional swagger when it came to these kinds of people. Even though he had come from the slums, his money had forced him to mingle amongst a more upscale group of individuals, which was his cliché, when it came to people that were resourceful.

"There they are," some female voices from the crowd yelled, as one of the girls that invited them came over to hug them and then the other two.

"Hey, beautiful," Javoo said while Cornelius grinned from ear to ear.

"Glad you could come. We have some champagne over here," Laura, the flight attendant said, as she grabbed Cornelius by the hand and led the way over to a table loaded with drinks.

"So, what's the occasion?" he asked as he turned and spotted a couple hug and kiss each other on the cheek.

"Well, here he is right here," Stephanie, the real estate girl, said as she reached out and grabbed the hand of a well dressed guy.

"This is a friend of ours. He's an attorney," the girl said.

"Hi, I'm Michael Walsh of Walsh and Associates Law Firm," the guy said as he shook Javoo's hand and then Cornelius's. They introduced themselves and then thanked him for welcoming them to the party.

"So this is the guy that owns the loft building. Nice place," Javoo said, sounding interested in one of the apartments.

"Yeah, now he owns a huge car lot," one of the girls said as she began to clap her hands, celebrating.

"A client of mine, a drug dealer, was murdered sometime last week and had a number of businesses," the man continued to say.

"I was able to gain ownership of one of his car lots. Funny thing, though. The guy leaves a good friend of his a record company. The label is up-and-coming, and may be looking at millions, and not even 30 minutes ago, I get a call from the guy who says he's turning the label over to some guy named Money Sack or Money Black; I can't recall his name, but I do know his last name was Williams. He's supposed to call me tomorrow morning," the lawyer said, giving them the whole scoop on his business.

Javoo and Cornelius looked at each other almost simultaneously. They knew exactly who the attorney was talking about. Money Black had to have been the one who killed Ralph, Cornelius thought, and he was hoping that Javoo was thinking the same thing.

The night was a smash. Cornelius had been snuggling up with Laura, while Javoo spoke with Stephanie about some homes he had been interested in around the city. It was now 2:30am and the party had finally shifted to one of the apartment houses in the building.

"Well, ladies, I better go," Javoo said as Marissa, the U.S. Customs girl, looked at him and started to insist on him staying a little while longer. Cornelius looked at him as well.

He knew that something was bothering him after he'd caught him in a stare off-and-on during the course of the evening.

"No really, I gotta go," he said as he hugged them and then walked out to his car.

"Call me tomorrow," Laura said to Cornelius as they both got into their cars and left.

Chapter Twelve

It was early Sunday morning and Chi-Chi was up doing some cleaning around the house. She wore a female's exercise top, a pair of shorts and house shoes, as she stood staring at a picture of her and her brother Ralph hanging on the wall in her living room. She had had a long day the day before, having to go to her brother's funeral, then sitting around to talk to people all afternoon. She had no intentions on going anywhere, turning on her stereo to the soothing sounds of Indie Arie, when her phone suddenly began to ring.

"Hello?" she quickly said after noticing that it was Cornelius calling her.

"Hey, how are you this morning?" he asked her.

"I'm fine," she responded.

"Come and let me take you to breakfast. I have to talk to you," he said to her.

"Ok, where do you want me to meet you?" Chi-Chi asked, kicking off her house shoes and then quickly went to slip into something she could go out in.

"Can you meet me at the Orleans? It's a spot just off of Main Street, down from the old Sears and the Fiesta. Do you know where it is?" he asked her.

"I think so. I'll call you if I have trouble finding it," she said and then hung up the phone. Chi-Chi was hoping that

Cornelius had some news for her. She had always liked him and had started to fall in love with him, until he and Javoo robbed her brother. As time passed, she had forgotten about him, and now it seemed that, due to the circumstances at hand, she had let bygones be bygones.

Cornelius leaned against his Cadillac CTS as he watched Chi-Chi back her car in next to his. He walked over to the driver's side and opened the door like a valet at a ballroom mansion. They hugged as if their relationship had been normal since they were last together.

"So, what's up?" she asked as they walked inside the place.

"I'm waiting on someone to show up. Someone who can put all this stuff together," he said to her. They placed their orders and went and sat at a table, as Cornelius spotted Javoo's Range Rover as it pulled into the parking lot.

"Here he comes now," he said to Chi-Chi, who was looking out of the window. She had never gotten a chance to meet Javoo.

Even the night that they robbed her brother, everything had happened so fast, she never really got a chance to see his face.

"Chi-Chi, this is Javoo; Javoo, this is Chi-Chi," Cornelius said as he introduced the two once Javoo came in and sat across the table from them. Javoo told her how he was sorry to hear about what had happened to her brother. He just felt like it was the right thing to say to a girl, who felt that she had no one else to go to about her brother's death.

"A guy named Money Black just might be the person responsible for what happened to your brother," Javoo said as Chi-Chi continued to listen.

"He's a dope dealer, a hustla from out on the Northside. He's one of those dudes that didn't like your brother too much because he was the competition. I beat him up one night at Carringtons Night Club a few years ago when he tried to disrespect me and some of my playa potnas," Javoo told her.

"So you know him," said Chi-Chi.

"Yeah, I know who he is. I hear about him from time to time," Javoo said and continued. "He has a guy named Mitchell who buys dope from him," he said as she looked at him.

"Okay, I saw him at the mall and he also came by my house the other night," she told him.

"Well, just this morning, the person your brother left the music business to turned the label, studio and all over to Money Black," Javoo said as he watched Chi-Chi's eye-brows frown.

"Smooth!" she said calling his name. Javoo went on to tell her how Money Black probably forced Smooth into giving up the record company and that all they needed to do was find out about the candy-blue Escalade that had been spotted at the bail bonds company.

"Money Black has a car and accessories shop out on the north. I know where it is. If that candy-blue Escalade is parked up there, then all the arrows point towards him. You can take what information you know to the police, as long as you keep me and Cornelius out of it," Javoo said, as he stopped to pay for their breakfast when an elderly lady walked up to the table. Chi-Chi couldn't believe what she was hearing. She didn't know Money Black, but everything she had just heard had

101

been discovered by the same person who had once robbed her brother; and it all added up like one plus one.

"Hold on," Chi-Chi said as she took out her cell phone to call Smooth. Javoo and Cornelius listened in as Smooth answered.

"How could you?" Chi-Chi asked Smooth sounding angry.

"How could you trade off something my brother left you? We just buried him yesterday and you done already let some nigga hustle you out of the record company," she said as if it had been all over the news.

Javoo and Cornelius could hear a tiny voice coming from Chi-Chi's cell phone as she started to breathe heavily and then hung up.

"So what did he say?" Cornelius asked her.

"He tried to say he didn't want to get rid if the company or somethin'. I just hung up," she said with a disgusting look on her face. Javoo's words had been 100% to her and now her mind was racing like a mad man's.

"Please help me repay this motherfucka!" she said, looking directly into Javoo's eyes and then Cornelius's. Javoo could see the frustration boiling inside her. She was more hurt than confused and was starting to get out of hand in the restaurant, so he thought that they had better go and talk somewhere a little more private. That's when they went outside and got inside his Range Rover to finish the conversation.

"Listen, Baby-girl. I can see that this is hurting you real bad. And if my boy didn't cut for you so much, I wouldn't be doin' this," he said as a sigh of relief filled Chi-Chi inside. Javoo began to discuss the details of helping her. He knew he had to think deep and, most of all, get her to understand some things she didn't know.

"Mitchell is no problem. We can handle him. We might can get him to talk if we can catch him slippin'. But Money Black is the slick one. He's got goons everywhere and he's got the money to make them move," he said. Javoo went on to explain to her about the businesses that Money Black had, the people that sold dope for him, and that he may even have a cop or two on his payroll.

"I have money, too," Chi-Chi said in a serious tone. "If I got to spend it all to get this motherfucka, I will," she said as her nostrils spread wide like a wild bull's.

"Well, if everything goes right, you won't have to," Javoo said back to her. He went on to tell her that he knew a real estate agent that could get her another place to stay right away. He told her that her life could be in danger because Money Black knew where she lived, and that with the type of money that she had, moving shouldn't be no problem.

* * *

Tracy came in early to open the store, after Shalon had called and told her that she wasn't feeling too good. She first took her things to the back, put on her nametag and then started to fill out some paperwork as the mall began to fill. That's when she noticed a tall, dark and handsome guy walk in and start looking around.

"Can I help you with anything?" she asked the guy.

"Yeah, I'm having trouble trying to find something for a very beautiful woman," the guy said back to her.

"Do you know her size?" asked Tracy. The guy looked her up and down, then back up again and said, "About your size."

Tracy began to smile. It was exactly what Javoo expected. He knew she didn't know who he was. She had never gotten the chance to meet him, so he wanted to go and see just how gullible she really was. That was his reason for having Shalon call in sick. He thought that he would go and run some game on her, while he had Shalon to drive out to Money Black's shop to look for the candy-blue Escalade. He also had Cornelius to keep an eye on Mitchell once they had left the restaurant that morning.

"Is Tracy your first or last name?" Javoo asked her.

"It's my first name," she said as she began to blush.

"Well, I've seen you in this mall several times and I happen to think that you are the most beautiful woman in the whole place. But I never said anything to you due to the fact that you are so pretty. There has to be some handsome prince," he said as Tracy continued to smile.

"Are you asking me if I have a man?" she asked. Javoo softly smiled and nodded. He was finally getting somewhere.

"Well, I do, but you know, for the past week, he hasn't been acting like a handsome prince," she said, giving him the assumption that she may be upset with Mitchell.

"Well, I'm not much of a thief at all, so I'm not tryin' to steal you. But if I could just borrow you for a few minutes, maybe we could have a casual drink or somethin'," he said to her. Tracy felt shy. She hadn't been approached by another man in a while and now this guy was making her feel whole again. She thought that Javoo did seem to be very sweet and respectable, and also charming at the same time. Those were the key elements it took to get a girl like her. Well, almost any girl.

"I could give you my number, you could call me later. I'm working by myself today, so I'm not able to take a break," she said to him.

"I could stay and help you," Javoo said, grabbing a woman's blouse and holding it up to his chest, making Tracy laugh. Some other women began to walk into the store. Tracy quickly wrote down her number and gave it to him.

"Well, I have to see to my customers; call me okay," she said as Javoo looked at her ass when she walked away. Tracy was definitely sexy. She looked like a young Vanessa Williams to him and as soon as he got the chance, he was gon' use her to make Mitchell burn.

Javoo left the mall and headed towards the Tanglewood Galleria area, just a few blocks away from where Tracy worked. He was going to meet Chi-Chi and Stephanie, the real estate chick he had just recently met, as he picked up his phone to call Cornelius.

"What's the deal?" Javoo asked as soon as Cornelius answered. "He's still in his condo with some freak," Cornelius told him.

"It ain't Shalon, is it?" Javoo asked. Both of them started to laugh.

"Naw, it ain't Shalon, but whoever it is, I see he still ain't learned his lesson," Cornelius said to him. Javoo told Cornelius he would meet him back at his apartment once he got through with Chi-Chi and Stephanie and then hung up. He then called Shalon to see if she had made it out to Money Black's shop.

"Hello," she answered.

"You go by there?" he asked her.

"I'm comin' up on the place now," she said.

"Look for a candy-blue Escalade, ok Baby?" he told her.

"Okay, I see some motorcycles, a BMW, a drop-top Benz and, oooh-oooh! Yeah, it's a candy-blue Escalade parked on the side of the building. I almost missed it," Shalon said with excitement.

"Good job. Now go on back home and I'll see you later," he said as he pulled up to where Stephanie was waiting. He hung up with Shalon and then stepped out of the rental he was in to give her a hug.

"So, where is she?" Javoo asked, not seeing Chi-Chi's yellow Corvette.

"She should be here any minute," Stephanie said. She told Javoo that she had a nice sky-rise apartment, with its own personal parking area, and at a nice price.

"She's gonna love it," Stephanie said, as they both saw Chi-Chi turn into the parking garage. Chi-Chi parked and then got out looking as fly as ever. She was rockin' yellow on yellow, which was somethin' most people couldn't rock with. She wore a yellow top, supported by a silver necklace with yellow diamonds in it. She had on a pair of silver-frame Dolce & Gabbana sunshades with yellow lenses, a pair of dark blue Apple Bottom jeans that had yellow stitching and yellow heels. Her fingernails and toenails were painted yellow and she even carried a yellow Coach handbag.

"Lookin' real fly today," Javoo said as Chi-Chi shook Stephanie's hand.

"I get my shine on from time to time," she said as she looked over her shoulder and cracked a smile at him. They both went up to check out the place that Stephanie had for her. It was beautiful, Chi-Chi thought, as she looked around. There was a fireplace, an island range cooking area, and the bathroom in the master bedroom had a Jacuzzi tub along with a stand up shower. The apartment even came with a wonderful view.

"I like this," she said as Stephanie opened the tall curtains to a window that showed all of downtown Houston. After showing Chi-Chi all the features of the apartment, Stephanie made a phone call to the owner, letting them know that they had a buyer.

"How soon can I move in?" Chi-Chi asked her.

"As soon as the deal is approved and the money is transferred from your account," Stephanie told her.

"What about the number to the security code?" she asked.

"I have it right here in my purse," Stephanie said as she dug the number out of her purse and gave it to her. Chi-Chi wanted to waste no time moving out of the house that she lived in. She didn't want to end up like her brother and especially by the same hands. Once they walked back down to their cars, Stephanie received a call from the owner letting her know that Chi-Chi was legit and that they appreciated her service.

"Ok, you're good to go. Here are the keys to the apartment and I hope you enjoy your new place," Stephanie said to Chi-Chi. Stephanie turned to give Javoo a huge hug. She thanked him and then told him that she owed him one just before she got in her car and left.

"So, where is Cornelius?" Chi-Chi asked Javoo and then reached into her purse and pulled out a few envelopes.

"I gotta go meet him back at his apartment when I leave here. We gotta move we need to make," he told her. Chi-Chi handed him the envelopes.

"What's this?" Javoo asked her.

"It's $20,000. It's just a little somethin' in case you need to buy some guns or any other equipment," Chi-Chi said.

Javoo looked at her. He could see that she wasn't playin' around in no shape, form nor fashion. The look of desperation was in her eyes and he really didn't want to ruin the better part of her day with the information Shalon had just given him, but he had to.

"It's been confirmed. A candy-blue Escalade is parked up at Money Black's shop right now," he told her. Chi-Chi immediately put her hand to her forehead and, began to think about her sister-in-law, Donna.

"Yeah, I know," Javoo patted her on the back and said, assuring her that something was going to be done. Javoo told her that he was gon' have Cornelius call her, as he walked her over to her car. He could imagine just how she was feeling. He could hear her press hard on the gas when she crunk up the Corvette and knew right then that she was hurt.

"Okay, mama, I gotcha," he said to himself, as he stood there with his arms crossed and watched her peel out of the parking garage.

* * *

Back at Cornelius' apartment, Javoo handed him an envelope as he stepped in the door.

"What's this?" Cornelius asked him.

"Oh, it's just a little advance from ya girl, Chi-Chi," he told him.

"Well shit, let's bust this down then," Cornelius said to him.

"Naw, that's yo' $10,000. I got my cut already," Javoo said. He sat down and began to tell him his plans, as far as them dealing with Money Black. He also told him that he really needed to catch up with Chi-Chi and spend some time with her. He knew that she still liked him, but he needed Cornelius to make sure.

"You know, we really got to gain her trust and make her really trust in us. We just need to do everything we can to keep her from thinkin' about that move we pulled on her brother, you know wudumsayin'," Javoo said, trying to stay two steps ahead of everything. He knew that if Cornelius went to her, she would give in. She was desperate, yes, but she was still vulnerable.

"You should go and spend the night with her at her new spot. It's nice, too," Javoo told him. The money Chi-Chi had given them was just a simple down payment. They already had everything they needed to make Money Black and Mitchell sweat, and that was Javoo's genuine ability to screw things up for them.

"So you think we can get Money Black?" Cornelius asked, sounding concerned.

"Man, we can only try. I mean, a million dollars is a lotta money, homey, but you know safety is our thang. No matter what happens, we have to survive the threat of goin' up against Money Black, and the chance of bumpin' into the police, so we gotta think smart and move fast," Javoo told him. "So what's gon' be our first move?" Cornelius asked as he stood ready, like a puppy wagging its tail.

"We gotta annoy this nigga. We gotta make him do some things he don't normally do," said Javoo.

"You mean rob him, right?"

"No, I mean burn him down," Javoo said with a burning desire in his eyes. Cornelius looked at him. He didn't seem to understand what he meant, but whatever it was, he was down with it.

"What about that nigga Mitchell?" Cornelius asked.

"We gotta catch up with him and Smooth. But first, we need to talk to Smooth, and that shouldn't be no problem," Javoo said with sure confidence.

Later that evening, Javoo finally got Shalon to calm down after he told her about the stunt that he pulled on Tracy. He had to get close to Mitchell and getting her to neglect him was the best way to stir him up. He told Shalon that he needed her to pretend to be an R&B singer so that they could get Smooth to come outside of Money Black's boundaries without making him suspicious.

He knew he wasn't gon' be hard to deal with as long as he and Chi-Chi could convince him that they were going to help him get the record company back. But that was just part of what Javoo had in store. His main focus was on the whereabouts of Money Black's stash, whether it was his drugs or his money. He felt that if he burned down his clothing store and his beauty & barber salon, it would limit some of his stash spots. And the studio, he knew too many niggas hung around that spot for Money Black to even think about hiding anything there. The only place he was gon' leave standing was the car and accessories shop. He knew he could keep a better eye on him that way. He also needed to know Money Black's real name and he was hoping that Stephanie could help him out with that. She did say she owed him a favor and he thought that maybe she could get her lawyer friend Mr. Walsh to give her Money Black's name and address, since Smooth had turned the record label, studio and all over to him.

* * *

Tracy's cell phone rang as she walked to her Nissan Murano and got in. She had been working all day and really just wanted to take a load off as she fastened her seat belt and turned the engine. She didn't notice the number in her phone and finally decided to take the call.

"Hello," she said as she answered.

"I don't know which is more beautiful, you or your voice," Javoo said, sounding like a true prince charming.

"Who is this?" she asked, sounding like a shy little girl.

"It's me, Romeo, the guy from the mall," Javoo said to her.

"You know, I was wondering if you were going to call," she said.

"As pretty as you are, you got to be kiddin' me," he said.

"Hey, you never did give me your name," Tracy quickly said.

"I'll tell you if you promise to come have a drink with me," said Javoo.

"Well, I'm about to leave the mall now. Where do you wanna meet?" she asked him. "Can you meet me at the Sky Bar? I'll be drivin' a white Mercedes," he said to her.

"Ok," Tracy said and then hung up. Everything that Shalon had told him about Tracy was true. She was gullible and most definitely square. Everything that he said tickled her. He felt that a few drinks might get her to open up and say some interesting things about Mitchell, especially with a little smooth-talk added. He had no problems when it came to dealing with women like Tracy, and Javoo had it in his mind to take her real fast.

Tracy had been working all day and knew she needed some relaxation. She was tired of working and then going straight home, while Mitchell stayed out until who knows when, if he even came home at all. She wanted to see what this new guy was all about and thought that it wouldn't hurt a bit just to have a few drinks.

She parked her Murano and then looked around to see if she could spot a white Mercedes. It was dark and just when she was about to pick up her phone to call him, she saw a white Mercedes pull into the valet section and park.

"Is that him?" she asked herself, hoping that it was. She could see Javoo step out and look in her direction, so she quickly got out and walked over to where he was standing.

"Nice car," she said, checking out his ride. Javoo's Mercedes wasn't anything like Mitchell's. It had an Asanti custom grill, TV screens in the head rest and a TV that came out of the dash. It wore no tint and it was sitting on a sparkling set of 22 inch Teflon rims. Tracy thought that Mitchell's S550 was clean, but Javoo's white-on-white S600 just said something to a woman. Something that made her think that she should be on the passenger side.

"So what's your name?" Tracy asked him.

"My name is Ladarian Walker," Javoo said, giving her a fake name.

"I feel kinda funny, meeting a strange guy like this," she said.

"Oh, I'm strange! Ok, I'll be that, but after tonight, I won't be," he said back to her, keeping his influence strong.

"Well, I guess that's why I'm here," said Tracy.

They went inside and had a few laughs. Everything was working out just as he had planned it. He had gotten her a little tipsy and got her to tell him everything she could about Mitchell. She told him about how Mitchell had been acting differently since last week, making Javoo wonder if he was with Money Black when Ralph and his wife were killed.

"The tough guy role huh?" Javoo said as he took another sip of his drink.

"Yeah! And I don't even know where all this is coming from. He's never acted like this before," Tracy said with a slur in her voice. Javoo also found out that Mitchell had started keeping his dope and money at her place, in so many words. The way that she explained to him how he would come in with his big duffle bags marinated in his head. Mitchell had made Tracy's apartment his nest, especially since they had robbed him.

During the course of the evening, Tracy had become hands on and everything with Javoo. Whenever he said something that was funny or something that was fly, she would lightly hit him. He knew then that he could have her. She was making it so easy for him, but the thought of Shalon kept on popping up in his head, and so he thought that he'd better just stick to the plan.

After Javoo and Tracy separated for the evening, Javoo met up with Cornelius back at his apartment. That's when Cornelius told him that he had already talked to Chi-Chi and that she had hired some people from a moving company to move her things into her new place. He also told him that she wanted him to come over later.

"That's what's up," Javoo said to him.

"But we gotta do one thing before you do," he quickly said, and then told Cornelius his plan. "We need somethin' we can knock a big window out with," Javoo said.

"I gotta baseball bat in my closet," said Cornelius.

"What about a gas can?" Javoo quickly asked.

"We can stop through the Trey and get one from some-body," Cornelius said.

They both figured that if they were going to go into Money Black's territory, they were going to need some protection, so it was already understood that takin' some heat wouldn't be such a bad idea. They didn't want to run into him or any of his people without having something to fight them off with, so they loaded up their clips, got in the rental that was parked at his apartment and went and found a gas can. They quickly stopped at a service station to fill the can up when Javoo got a call from Stephanie.

"Hey, Stephanie," Javoo said as he answered.

"Hey, I got that information you called and asked me about," she said as she continued.

"The guy you asked about name is Eric Dywane Williams. He has two addresses; one off of Highway 6 and I-10, at 2727 Hathaway Drive, apartment number 5. I checked it out. It's a condo that he's had for three years. The other is out in Katy, a gated community with houses ranging from $300,000 and up, on 604 Lampoon Street," Stephanie said, giving Javoo every-thing she could find out about Money Black.

"Okay, Stephanie, I appreciate that," he told her.

"Well, I did owe you one. That's the least I could do," she said back to him. They both had hung up just in time. Javoo had exited the freeway and was heading for the place Money Black had as a clothing store. It was around 11:30 at night and the parking lot was totally empty.

"There it is right there," Cornelius said as he pointed at a store that was located on the far end of a small shopping center on Antoine Boulevard. Javoo wanted to waste no time. He reached into the back seat and grabbed the baseball bat, while Cornelius grabbed the gas container. They got out, walked up to the front of the clothing, took a quick look around and with one solid swing, Javoo smashed the front glass of the place. Cornelius quickly ran in and started tossing gas everywhere, then Javoo immediately sent the place into flames.

"Let's go!" Javoo said as they quickly got back in the car and sped away.

Chapter Thirteen

Money Black sat at a truck stop, waiting on his latest drop from his Dominican connection. They had been his supplier for a while now and he was quite comfortable with the way that the Dominicans did their business. They would always have an SUV already parked at the truck stop, and all he had to do was have somebody to pull up with the money, get out of that car and into the SUV that would already have the keys in it, while he sat back and watched, just as the Dominicans would do. He would always have two cars to trail him in any case the deal went bad. His once a week fa-sho plug had always been on top of their business, but on this night the Dominicans had not made it and he was starting to feel nervous.

"Where these motherfuckas at?" he said as he eye-balled every single SUV in sight. He was sitting in an all-black Chevy Tahoe, with dark tinted windows, along with his younger brother C-Dub, and one of his boys, when his cell phone suddenly began to ring. It was his grandmother.

"Hey Grandma," he said as he answered.

"Boy, I just got a call from the Houston Fire Department's Fire Chief," the old woman said as Money Black listened to her. "The store done somehow caught on fire and burned to the ground," she told him.

"WHAT?!" Money Black screamed in frustration.

"I don't know what happened, 'cause you know I'm always here in my livin' room," said the old woman.

"Ok, Grandma, I'll go and check it out," he said and then hung up. Money Black had put the clothing store in his grandmother's name just last year, in case the feds ever tried to seize the place, due to his affiliation with the streets.

"Damn!" he said, slamming his phone into the console. He really needed to leave, but the Dominicans had just pulled into the truck stop.

"Bout fuckin' time," he said. Everything went as it usually did. An SUV was parked with 40 kilos of cocaine and 30-pounds of meth inside it, and another with 350 pounds of hydro marijuana parked right next to it.

"Ok, fellas, let's do this real quick, and get on back. Somethin' just came up," Money Black said, speaking into the radio on his cell phone.

A car with the money was left for the Dominicans, who would be sure to contact him if he was short of any funds. He didn't want to ever risk the chance of them coming to look for him, and so he knew his best bet was to always stay on top of what he had to do when it came to dealing with the Dominicans.

After talking to his grandmother again, Money Black wondered what kind of fool would do something like this to his clothing store. Everybody knew him and he had not made any new enemies. Well, at least he thought he didn't. But for someone to deliberately burn his store down stained his brain, like a hot horseshoe branding a cow's ass, and he wanted to know what the deal was. But first, he had to take care of some more major business, and so the used-to-be clothing store would just have to wait.

* * *

Chi-Chi had been busy hanging up pictures and curtains all around her new place after she had finally gotten everything situated. It was late and she started to yawn when her cell phone suddenly began to ring. "Haah, hello," she yawned and answered.

"Hey, I was just callin' to check up on you," Cornelius said.

"I see you finally decided to call," she said to him.

"Well, we had some work to do, if you know what I mean," he said, as he and Javoo pulled up in front of his apartment.

"So where are you now?" she asked him.

"I just made it to my apartment, but I was about to leave again," he told her.

Chi-Chi started to tell him how she felt like he had been avoiding her in her time of need, and that she thought he would have spent more time with her since she first called him.

"I haven't been avoiding you, Chi-Chi. Besides, I was really on my way to see you. That's where I was going," Cornelius said and then cracked a short laugh.

"Stop playin', Cornelius," she said, thinking he was about to hit the streets.

"Girl, you know I wanna see you. Especially since I saw you get out of your car at the Smoke Shop, lookin' all sexy, until you started snottin' all over my ride," he said making fun of her.

"Shut up!" she said, sounding shy and embarrassed at the same time.

"So, are you comin' or what?" she asked him.

"Yeah, I'm comin'. Just let me grab a few things first though, ok?" he said.

Cornelius arrived at Chi-Chi's new sky-rise apartment 20 minutes later. He couldn't believe that this was actually happening. He thought, "How could a person forgive some-one, who had done such an awful thing to her and her family?" Even though what he and Javoo had done was now behind them, he still couldn't get it out of his mind, and tonight, he was going to tell her how he really was feeling.

He knocked on the door and waited for her to answer.

"Hey," she said as he walked in.

"Oh, ok! I really do dig this spot," Cornelius said as he took a quick look around her place.

"Yeah, I like it, too, but I haven't had the chance to put it together like I want it yet," she said as Cornelius followed her into the kitchen area.

"You smell like gas," she quickly said, waving her hand to get rid of the smell.

"Yeah, I know," he said.

"You want somethin' to drink? I only got a few sodas, some orange juice and some water for right now," she said.

"Naw, I'm cool. I really just wanted to take a shower before I do anything else," Cornelius said, unzipping the bag that he brought with him. Chi-Chi showed him to the walk-in shower, gave him a couple of towels and then turned on some soft music. He began to get undressed while she went through a few boxes to look for something more comfortable to put on. He stepped into the shower and started to soap up a small wash cloth, when the door to the shower suddenly opened and Chi-Chi stepped in.

"What are you doin'? I thought I was the one that smelled like gas," he said as his dick immediately started to rise at the site of Chi-Chi's naked body.

"You want me to get out?" she asked, grabbing the soapy towel in one hand and his hard dick in the other. Cornelius could only let out a low sigh, as he felt the warm water running down his back and the softness of Chi-Chi's hand on his dick.

"I have to tell you somethin'," he said as she continued to rub the soapy towel all over him.

"When you first met me, I was young and kinda wild. I didn't have time to think about the things that I was doin'. I was livin' day-to-day, and when I met you, I really wanted to be with you. That night at your brother's house was a spur-of-the-moment thing. I knew that I was makin' a big mistake, but I didn't have no money, my mama was livin' in a fucked up spot, and I was just tryin' to make things better, until Javoo showed me how to get money and hold on to it. Since then a lot about me has changed. I thought about you every day, but I felt like you just didn't want to have nothin' to do with me. I'm sorry for what happened that night and I'm sorry for what happened to your brother," Cornelius said as he stared into her eyes.

A tear slowly came out the corner of Chi-Chi's eye and blended with the shower water on her face. What Cornelius had said touched her and she believed him. They started to kiss as they stood there with the shower water running between them.

"I hated you after that night," she said, looking into his eyes. "But why did I miss you so much?" she quickly asked as Cornelius reached under her arms and lifted her up against the wall of the shower.

Chi-Chi raised her legs up as Cornelius slid his dick inside her.

"I missed you, too," he said as he stroked her 135-pound frame. She was like a feather to him. Her body was soft and light enough to carry, her pussy wet, and nipples pressed hard against his chest as she held him tightly around his neck. Chi-Chi was soundless. It was like her heart had stopped, but her body was still responding to his movements.

"Ahhh!" Chi-Chi sighed. She had finally made a sound.

"You want me to stop?" he asked her.

"No! Please don't," she said and then grabbed his face with both hands and stuck her tongue in his mouth. Cornelius began to fuck her a little faster, as Chi-Chi's light frame continued to slide back and forth on him, milking him like a suction pump.

"I want you back," she said as she looked at him.

"I'm already back," he said fucking her harder. Chi-Chi wrapped her legs around his waist and clamped down on him.

She could feel his body start to tighten up and his dick, hard as a rock throbbing inside her.

"Ooooh! You gon' make me cum, Cornelius," she said with her eyes bucked-wide open.

"I'm already cummin'," he said as he froze up like a statue. Her body trembled as they stood there holding each other.

They kissed. It was what they both had wanted. To make up.

"Come on, let's get out," Cornelius said and then opened the shower door to let her out first. They dried off and got into bed. It was late and, to him, it had turned out to be a very rare night. He had finally gotten the chance to tell her what was on his mind, and now all he could do was hold her until they both fell asleep.

Chi-Chi woke up the next morning feeling like a brand new woman. She had cooked a nice turkey bacon, eggs and waffles breakfast and was getting some orange juice out of the fridge, when Cornelius came and sat at the table.

"So what's on your mind?" she asked as she looked at him.

"Last night, me and Javoo burned down one of Money Black's stores," he told her. Chi-Chi put her hand over her mouth, surprised at what he had just said. She didn't know that they were going to take that kind of action against Money Black.

"Boy! No wonder you smelled like gas last night," she said as Cornelius began to tell her what their next plan was going to be.

"I need you to give me Smooth's number, ok? Javoo has somebody that's gonna call him. When this person gets in touch with Smooth, Javoo is gon' come and pick you up, so y'all can talk to him. We just don't want anybody to see you or Javoo, you know wudumsayin?"

Chi-Chi nodded her head yes as Cornelius continued to tell her the plan. "After we catch up with Smooth, we gon' deal with this nigga, Mitchell," Cornelius told her.

"You mean the guy that came by my house?" she asked.

"Yeah. If Javoo found out what he needed to last night, then we'll know what to do. If he knows anything he'll tell us," he said, assuring her that they were going to get down to the bottom of everything. Chi-Chi gave Cornelius a kiss. She was glad that they had got back together again and she was feeling good about what they were doing. It had been a long time since they had last saw each other. Now, they weren't just lovebirds again; they were feeling like a team.

Chapter Fourteen

Tracy and Mitchell had had an hour-long argument the night before. She had come home feeling a little tipsy and really wasn't in the mood to hear him whining about her not coming straight home from work or about his homeboy's clothing store being burned down. She just didn't care what he was talking about or what he had to say. All she knew was that he wasn't making her feel anything like this new guy did. They had argued so much that she decided to sleep on the couch, while Mitchell slept in her bed.

"All you wanna do is run the streets," she said as Mitchell stepped out of her bedroom, fully dressed and with a small backpack slung over his shoulder.

"I'm gettin' tired of this shit," she said, holding her head with a half-ass hang over.

"I don't know what the hell is wrong witchu. You must be still drunk from last night," Mitchell said to her.

"Yeah, whatever!" she said back to him.

"I just know that when I come back here this evening, you better have yo' mind right," he told her and then slammed the door behind him. Tracy struggled to pull herself together. She hadn't got that drunk in a long time, but she had to get up and get ready for work. She thought about Shalon and wondered why she had not heard from her in the past couple of days. She

125

didn't know that the plot Javoo had against Mitchell would cause her to have an attitude or that he was only peeling her for information.

Tracy had finally managed to take a shower and get dressed. She forced herself to eat a bowl of cereal and then hit the door and headed for work. She was wishing that she could just call in, but she had too much paperwork to do and didn't want to leave Shalon strained up.

"What's up girl?" Tracy said to her.

"Heeey!" Shalon said as if the cat had gotten her tongue. Shalon looked at Tracy like she had already slept with Javoo. "So whatchu been doin'?" she asked Tracy. "Not too much. Just takin' care of a little business," Tracy responded.

"Ah! You been seein' somebody, huh girl?" Shalon asked as she gave her a fake smile. Shalon wanted to know what was really going on. She figured that since Tracy was so lame, she could easily pick her. Tracy smiled. She just couldn't hold it in. She had to tell Shalon about the guy she had met.

"Girrrl, I met this tall, dark, handsome guy," she said, sounding like she had won a prize. "He has a white Mercedes, just as clean as Mitchell's, and he's straight up. Doesn't seem like he's out to play no games," she said with a sincere look on her face. Shalon was on fire. Her chest burned inside and her stomach was starting to turn. She had never even seen Javoo's Mercedes, and now her friend was standing there bragging about her lover's ride right to her face.

"You slept with him yet?" asked Shalon.

"No girl, of course not. I just met him," said Tracy.

"Well, I have a doctor's appointment today at 2 o'clock, so I'm gon' have to leave for a little while," Shalon told her. Cornelius had already called and given her Smooth's number, but when she called him, he didn't answer. She had ended up leaving him a message saying that she would like to meet with him so that he could listen to some tracks she had been recording lately and was hoping that he would get back to her soon enough. She really wanted to see Javoo, though. She was mad as hell at him and once 2 o'clock finally came around, she didn't waste no time going to the break room to grab her purse.

"Tracy, I'll be back, ok?" Shalon said as she left the store.

* * *

Smooth called Shalon just as she pulled out of the Galleria and told her to come to the studio, but she told him that it was too far and that she didn't want to be late for work. She then asked him if he could meet her in the parking lot of the *This Is It* soul food restaurant out in mid-town, and Smooth agreed to meet her there. He had no problems when it came to music, but meeting a girl at a soul food restaurant sounded like a date to him, especially a girl that was proclaiming to be an R&B singer.

He had been fairly upset with the way Money Black had handled him, but at least he was still alive. He had already gotten half of a million dollars from him and was supposed to get another $500,000 on a later date; that is, if he was still going to be president of the company. He had not gotten the chance to work with an R&B singer before, and he felt like this could be his big break. That' s when he picked up his phone and called to see if Shalon had made it to the restaurant.

"Hello!" Shalon said as she answered.

"So, what are you driving?" he asked.

"I'll be in a Range Rover," she told him.

"Ok, I'll just get in with you and see whatchu workin' with," Smooth said and then they both hung up. When he turned into the parking lot, he noticed that there were only a couple of vehicles parked there. A Nissan Titan truck was parked right at the entrance next to a pearl-colored Cadillac Escalade and he could see a Range Rover sitting in the shade of a huge tree that was standing next to the parking lot. He pulled his Porsche in next to the Range Rover, got out and then quickly got in on the passenger side. Shalon was sitting in the driver's seat and when he looked in the back, he was spooked when he laid his eyes on Chi-Chi and another guy sitting next to her. That's when his shoulders dropped. He knew he had been tricked.

"I know you're surprised to see me, but we had to do it this way. We're just trying to keep everything low key," Chi-Chi said as she looked at him.

"Low key!"

"Yeah, low key," Javoo said as Smooth looked at him.

"Do you know who I am? Do you remember me?" Javoo asked him.

"Nah! Where I'm supposed to know you from?" asked Smooth.

"A few years ago, you and Money Black were at Carrington's night club. I was the one that beat him up, and instead of

128

gettin' up off his ass to fight back, he hit you," Javoo said as Smooth nodded his head, now remembering the night that happened.

"Oh yeah, I remember that night," he said.

"Well, here's the deal. We feel that Money Black forced you to turn that record company over to him," Javoo said.

"Yeah! That son of a bitch broke into my house and threatened to kill me. I had to," said Smooth.

"We also feel that he had somethin' to do with Ralph and his wife's murder," Javoo said as Smooth's eyes got big. Ralph was his boy, and he had promised himself that if he ever ran across the person that was responsible for Ralph's death, he was gon' do somethin' to 'em. Now that he knew it could be Money Black, he had to think twice. He knew he wasn't stiff enough to face him, not by his self.

"Do you want that company back?" Chi-Chi asked him.

"Hell yeah, because he maybe about to make a lotta money; money that me and Ralph worked hard for," Smooth told her.

"Well, I'm gon' help you get it back, but we, me and you, gon' go 50/50 on it. Is that a deal?" Chi-Chi asked him.

"You damn right it's a deal," said Smooth.

"Money Black gon' pay for what he done, but what we are here to find out is do you want to help us?" Javoo asked him.

"What do I have to do? Just tell me and I'll do it," Smooth said as he looked at both of them.

"We might need you to help us find out where he keeps his stash. I'm talkin' about his drugs or money; it don't matter. Any information you can give us will help. We gotta try to find a way to hurt him. Since you are the president of the label, he might trust you a little more than anyone else," Javoo said to him.

"That nigga don't trust nobody. He might trust his lil' brother, but I don't think he even knows where the nigga live," said Smooth.

"Don't worry about that. I already know that he's got two spots, and I'm gon' go check 'em out soon enough," Javoo said.

"What about this nigga Mitchell?" Chi-Chi asked as Shalon's eyes got big as well.

Mitchell's name was the last thing she thought she woulda heard in that kind of a conversation, and she wanted to hear what he had to do with what they were talkin' about. She had already been looking at Chi-Chi and was starting to think that she had saw her somewhere before.

"I don't really know him, but I do know who he is. Here lately, he's been kinda hangin' around the studio. He's one of Money Black's boys," Smooth told them. Javoo went on to tell him how he planned to get Money Black. He also told him that he should think about finding a new place to stay, especially after he had told them how Money Black had poured gas all over him and his furniture and threatened to burn him alive.

"Well, you got my number, call me," Chi-Chi said, tapping Smooth on his shoulder.

"I will, just promise me you gon' deal with this nigga," Smooth said as he looked at Javoo.

"Oh he gon' get dealt with. I put that on everythang," Javoo said to him.

"Ok then," Smooth said as he nodded his head at Shalon, got out of the Range Rover and back into his car. He felt like a thousand pounds had been lifted off of his shoulders. He had been wanting to make up with Chi-Chi so bad since she had last called him and he was glad he had finally got the chance to talk to her. He also knew that this guy Javoo was probably the only person that wasn't afraid of Money Black. He had seen what he could do that night in the club and he was hoping he could do the same thing to help him get that record label back.

Getting the people that were responsible for Ralph's death would be one of the best things that happened in a long time, and if he was going to have anything to do with it, he was gon' make sure Money Black paid for everything that he done.

* * *

Shalon rode with Javoo back to Cornelius's apartment where her car was parked. She couldn't wait for him to get off the phone so she could talk to him about what was going on with him and Tracy.

"Okay, what's the matter now?" he asked once he finally hung up.

"Tracy acts like she's in love, Nigga, that's what the matter is," Shalon said with a grouchy attitude. "I already have to put up with you being married, and that's only because you was already married when we met. But this is supposed to be my homegirl, Javoo. Why you doin' this to me?" she asked with an aching tone.

"Look baby! Chi-Chi is talkin' about payin' me and Cornelius a million dollars if we can get this nigga Money Black. And if I'm right, we gon' end up gettin' a whole lot more than that, so you just be cool, alright? I know what I'm doin'. I promised you that I wasn't gon' touch Tracy, and I'm tryin' to make sure all of us stay safe through this whole thing, you know wudumsayin'?" Javoo said, trying to calm her attitude.

Shalon sat back in her seat and crossed her arms, as she felt the cool breeze coming from the vent of the Range Rover. She knew she couldn't stop him from doing what he was doing. Javoo was way too much for her and that was what she loved about him. He was a street soldier, a take charge kinda guy that seemed to know every corner of the universe.

Cornelius thought about Chi-Chi as he took her to check on her record shop and the apartment complex that she owned. Everything was looking good as far as business was concerned. She had definitely been blessed and now as he looked at her, he couldn't help but to think about what Javoo had told him. There had to be a reason why she was brought back into his life, he thought.

It was like it was meant to be. Javoo had told him that he needed to take a good look at what he had standing before him and the life that was now behind him. She was rich and had her own businesses, a street thug's dream. He also told him that there was no way the street life was going to last forever and for him to think about that when it came to his own life. And then he told him he was gon' think the same thing about his own, but for now, this last job had to be done.

Chapter Fifteen

It was just past 9 o'clock pm when Money Black looked at his watch. He had been waiting on Mitchell to come and get his work when his phone suddenly began to ring.

"Hey Gloria," he answered.

"Money Black! Money Black!" Gloria cried over the phone. Gloria was a professional hair stylist he had hired to run his beauty and barber salon. She had taken the place and worked wonders with it, not to mention the clientele that poured its way in once the doors were open.

"The place is on fire," the woman continued to cry.

"You gotta be kiddin' me," he said, not believing the events over the past two days. Money Black quickly grabbed his car keys and headed out the door of his car shop.

"I'ma fuck somebody up!" he said as he got in his car, crunk it up and sped towards his salon, which was only a few blocks away.

When he got there, he couldn't believe his eyes. Black smoke was pouring out of his place. He could hear the sirens of the fire trucks coming, but it was too late.

"I'm gon' find out who's doin' this," he mumbled. But who could it be, he thought? Maybe Ralph had some closer friends than he thought but, then again, he felt like they woulda burned down the studio before any other place. He knew

Smooth was too soft and too scary to do something like that. Then he thought about some of the youngsters that hung around the studio. Maybe one of them was starting to trip over the loss of Ralph and was out for revenge on his own. He just couldn't put it together. He picked up his phone and dialed up the numbers to each and every person that surrounded him and told them to meet him at his car and accessories shop, asap. He mentioned the fact that someone was burning down his businesses, and if they didn't show up, he was gon' label them as a suspect.

Everybody that Money Black could think of sat in the back of his car and accessories shop. They were lined all along the wall as he stood, walking on top of his pool table, like he was a modern day Nino Brown.

"If there's anybody in this room that can tell me anything about what's happenin' to my shit, now's the time to let me know," he said as he breathed heavily. The room was silent. No one moved or made any gestures. Smooth sat along the wall and watched the pain that Money Black was suffering come right through his skin. He loved it, seeing him with his back against the wall.

"I got a hundred thousand dollars to the person who can find out who's burnin' down my shit-a hundred thousand!" he said, sounding like a Don. Everybody started to look back and forth at each other. There was a lot of money being offered and not one of them knew nothin'. Money Black was starting to feel kinda weird. He was almost certain that somebody woulda said somethin' or at least pulled him to the side, after hearing that kinda number.

"Look-out, Mitchell!" he said as everybody started to leave the room. Mitchell stopped to see what he wanted. He had come to pick up his product, but now it seemed that Money Black was wanting him to do something else.

"Yeah, what's up," he asked.

"I might need you to make another move for me," Money Black said to him. Mitchell was starting to feel like he was Money Black's right hand man. He had not only been ordered to kill two people, he was sent on private missions as well.

"What's that?" he asked Money Black.

"I need you to take another ride over to lil' mama's house again. I think she might know somethin' about this," he said as Mitchell looked at him.

"You know, this shit didn't start happenin' until we fucked off her brother. Now I own that record company, so it ain't no tellin' what this bitch got up her sleeve. Smooth's ho'-ass mighta mentioned somethin' that's got her trippin'," Money Black told him.

"So, you want me to go and talk to her again?" asked Mitchell. Money Black looked him up and down. He had the same look on his face that he had when they killed Ralph.

"Yeah, nigga! Talk to the bitch. I don't care how you do it, just see if the bitch knows anything," Money Black said as Mitchell nodded his head and headed for the door.

Mitchell rode by Chi-Chi's old house, slowly observing the home real estate sign sitting in the front yard. The house was dark and had no curtains hanging from the windows.

"This bitch done moved!" he said to himself as he drove on by. He called Money Black and told him that she had moved out of the house, and that's when Money Black told him that she had a small record shop and for him to check for her there the following day. He drove on thinking about Tracy and how she had been acting lately. He had tried to call her earlier, but got no answer. It wasn't like her not to answer his call. He knew she had always been head-over-heels for him, but now she was acting kinda strange.

He quickly looked in his review mirror and then back at the road, wondering if he was still attractive. His good looks and the way he dressed had always won her over, but he knew it was his presence that was most important.

He picked up his cell phone and tried her home number. There was no answer. He then decided to call her cell phone and still got no answer.

"Where this bitch at?" he asked himself as he drove on. He knew she would usually make it home shortly after the mall would close, but for the past couple of nights she had been doing some things that she didn't normally do. She had been staying out drinking and was starting to talk crazy to him whenever she did come in. She'd slept on the couch and now she wasn't even answering any of his calls. He frowned. Something was going on with her, but he just didn't know what it was. He then thought about Shalon and that maybe Tracy had went over to her spot for a little while. He didn't know where Shalon lived and he knew he couldn't just call there. How would that look to Tracy, he thought? Suddenly, his cell phone began to ring. It was one of his local customers wanting to meet with him on a deal, and so he was gon' have to catch up with Tracy later. It was time for business.

* * *

Smooth called Chi-Chi the very next morning and told her all about the meeting that Money Black had at his car shop. He insisted that she needed to be careful and then told her how he and Young Thug, one of the artists from the label, had been just lounging around the studio sampling some music, when the youngster told him that Money Black had taken him out to a big fancy house out in Katy, where he offered him some money and some dope if he needed it until his album dropped.

"So you think he could be holding all of his drugs and money there?" Chi-Chi asked Smooth.

"Maybe, maybe not," he said. Chi-Chi didn't know nothing about no drugs, or actually never knew the movements of a person that did. But at this particular time, she wanted to find Money Black's nest. She knew she wasn't the street type, so she began to think that she should just let Javoo and Cornelius handle the street stuff and try to find a way to help Smooth get that record company back.

"Ok, I'll call Javoo and tell him what you told me. In the meantime, I'ma try to make a couple phone calls to check up on somethin', so I'll holla atcha later," she said and then hung up. Chi-Chi found the number to Mr. Walsh's law firm and forwarded the call. She wanted to know the legal procedure it took to get the record company back and listened as the lawyer's secretary put her through.

Michael Walsh speaking," the man said once he answered.

"Hi, Mr. Walsh, this is Chitora Hastings," she said.

"Well, hello Chitora. How can I help you?" he asked her.

"I'm calling because I wanted to talk to you about the record company my brother had," she told him.

"Yes, you mean the one that Mr. Williams now owns," he said.

"Yeah, what can I do to get that company? What's the process?" she asked the man.

"What? Did something happen to him also?" he asked her.

"No, but me and the guy my brother first left the label to may want to try to purchase it again," she told him.

"I didn't understand why he turned it over to him in the first place," said Mr. Walsh.

"Well, there was a huge misunderstanding. We're going 50/50 in on it this time," she told him.

Mr. Walsh explained to her all of the proper procedures she needed to take to get the record company back. He told her that he would fax her some papers that would need to be signed by the owner, if she could get his signature, and that was all she needed to hear.

"Ok, you can fax me at my record shop," she said and then gave him her fax number. She hung up the phone and waited for the fax to come through. When she received the paperwork, she called Cornelius and told him to come over to the record shop.

* * *

Cornelius called and told Javoo everything that Smooth and Mr. Walsh had told Chi-Chi as he spoke to him on his cell phone. He told him how Chi-Chi had been surprised to see Shalon in his Range Rover after seeing her in the mall, which was also a surprise to the both of them as well. They didn't know what was going to surprise them next, but they had already gone too far to be worrying about coincidences, and now Javoo was wanting to fill Chi-Chi in on some more of his plan.

"Ok, I'm gon' have lunch with Shalon today, so you and Chi-Chi should meet us at the Cactus Grill, next to the 610 freeway," Javoo told him.

"Ok, I'm on my way to see her at her record shop now. We'll be there," Cornelius said and then they hung up. Cornelius began to smile as he turned into the parking lot of the record shop. He could see that Chi-Chi had decided to drive her brother's Aston Martin that morning, and he was glad to see that she was feeling better by the minute. She had really been taking the things that had been happening since her brother's death kinda hard and he was proud to know that their plan against Money Black was coming together.

He parked his Cadillac CTS next to the Aston Martin and got out. He didn't even get to make it to the door before Chi-Chi rushed out to give him a hug.

"Good mornin', baby," he said.

They kissed and then went inside. When he told her that they were going to have lunch with Javoo and Shalon, she started to think of how small the world was, first seeing Shalon at the mall when she went to pick up something for her brother's wake and then actually sitting in Javoo's Range Rover with her. She thought about everything. She thought about how Javoo and Money Black met, and then about Mitchell after seeing him at the mall and at her house. She even thought about Shalon working with Mitchell's girlfriend, too. It was all like a mystery, she thought as she ran her fingers through her hair.

"What's wrong baby?" he asked her.

"This is crazy! Everything is just fucking crazy," she said, feeling like the streets were full of demons.

"Maybe you'll feel a lot better if you got a bite to eat, so c'mon," he said, grabbing her by both hands and pulling her out of the chair she was sitting in. Cornelius leaned back in the passenger side of the Aston Martin, checkin' out the interior and the sleek design of the car's dash.

"This a sweet ride," he said as Chi-Chi floored the car out onto the freeway and headed back towards the south side of town.

"Yeah, I been likin' it ever since my brother first bought it," she said just before he told her how he and Javoo had set Money Black's beauty and barber salon on fire the night before. Chi-Chi started to laugh.

"Not again!" she said still laughing. They pulled into the parking lot of the Cactus Grill's restaurant, where Javoo and Shalon sat patiently waiting. They had not noticed the white Lincoln MKS with dark tinted windows that was following them. They all got out and shook hands with each other, as Chi-Chi and Shalon briefly hugged and then they all went inside.

Mitchell frowned at the sight of Shalon when he saw her in the parking lot of the restaurant. Money Black had asked him to check Chi-Chi out, just to see what kind of moves she was making, and now he was seeing both her and Shalon together.

"What the fuck is goin' on?" he said to himself, thinking of the robbery. First, he thought about him being robbed while Shalon lay next to him, crying like she was really scared. Now, she was in the same company as Chi-Chi and that didn't add up.

"This roach-ass bitch!" he said, feeling more aggravated than before. Shalon was in too many places and around too many people. People that seemed to be against him and Money Black, he thought. He looked at the two guys that was with them and couldn't tell if they were the same two that robbed him or not. The ones that had robbed him wore masks, so it was almost impossible to blame them without noticing something about them. He just figured that they were two guys that was trying to smash a couple freaks, and then picked up his cell phone to call Money Black.

"Talk to me!" Money Black said answering his phone.

"Man, I got up this morning and went to check out Ralph's sister like you asked me to, and guess who I saw with her?" Mitchell asked him.

"I don't know. Hit me with the hot track, Nigga," said Money Black.

"Well, Ralph's sister and some nigga go to a restaurant out on the Southside. That's when she met up with the same bitch that was with me when I got robbed," Mitchell said to him.

"Oh yeah? Now that's some news we both could use," said Money Black.

"Yeah, they had some other nigga wit 'em, too, but I couldn't tell if they were the ones that robbed me or not," Mitchell said to him.

"You know what? We might need to catch that bitch, 'cause I bet she know somethin'," he told Mitchell.

"Well, she works at the mall with my girl, Tracy," said Mitchell.

"We might can't get her there. We don't want nobody to see us. You gotta get'cha girl to tell you where she live at, or we can follow her and just hope she stops somewhere, so we can catch her slippin'," Money Black said. After they hung up, Mitchell thought about how Tracy had been acting. He needed to set her straight anyway, so he just knew she was gon' tell him where Shalon lived.

Chapter Sixteen

Tracy noticed that Mitchell's car was already parked in the parking garage when she pulled in. She smirked her lips, knowing that it wasn't like him to be home so early. She was used to him coming in at all times of the night and wondered why this day was suddenly different from all of the other days. That's when she thought about wanting to see Javoo. She had not heard from him all day. She thought that maybe he woulda called before she made it home, but she guessed he had better things to do as she parked her Murano, got out and took the stairs up to her apartment.

"Hey!" she said as she walked in.

"I gotta talk to you," Mitchell roughly said. Tracy wasn't in the mood for an argument. She thought that he was still upset about her coming in late the night before and wanted to fuss about it.

"I don't wanna argue with you," she said, throwing up her hand as she attempted to walk by him towards her bedroom.

"I need you to tell me where Shalon live," he said, gritting his teeth and grabbing her arm to spin her around.

"What is wrong with you?" she asked, feeling the seriousness in Mitchell's grip on her arm.

"I'ma ask you again, where Shalon live at?" he asked her.

"Why you wanna know where she live?" Tracy asked him.

143

"Just tell me where the girl live, that's all I ask," he said.

"That's none of your business," she said back to him.

Mitchell slapped Tracy down to the floor.

"I'm tired of yo' smart-ass mouth, bitch, now tell me where she live," he said as he stood over her.

"Get the hell out, Mitchell! Get out!" she screamed. She had not seen Mitchell act like this before and thought that she better do something before the situation got worse.

"I'm callin' the police," she said and then tried to scramble over to the phone.

"Bitch, you ain't callin' nobody!" he said as he grabbed her and slammed her against the wall, holding his hand tightly to her throat. Tears began to come from Tracy's eyes. She had never expected this to happen, especially the way that he was handling her.

"Where she live at?" he yelled with his hand pressed hard to her neck. "She stay in Greenhouse Patio, off Airport Boulevard," she said as she cried.

"What's her apartment number?"

"605," she said as she slid down the wall still crying. She watched as Mitchell went into the closet, came out and walked towards the door with two large duffle bags. He knew he could not afford to leave all of the drugs and money he had lying around her apartment, not after what he had just done. He looked back at her, snatched his keys from the bar in the living room and then slammed the door behind him when he left.

"Sorry ass punk!" Tracy said as she sat there on the floor in a trance. She couldn't believe what had just happened. Mitchell had put his hands on her in the worse way in her book but still, she just couldn't see herself sending him to jail. She knew it would just make things worse. He had a lot of money put into her account and she knew he would be coming back for it whenever he got out. But that still didn't explain what he wanted with Shalon, she thought. She got up off the floor, walked over to her cordless phone and called Shalon's number. Her answering machine picked up, so she left her a message to call her as soon as she could .

"I wonder what he want with her?" she said to herself, knowing that he wanted Shalon for something, and whatever it was, it was serious.

* * *

Javoo woke up early the next morning feeling drained of all his energy. He and his wife Tanasia had made love half the night, and now she was already gone for the morning.

"I don't see how she could do it," he said, pulling himself out of bed, feeling as weak as a bum with a million dollar hangover. He knew that Tanasia loved being up at the children's center. There was nothing that could keep her away from those kids, not even himself, he thought, as he took a long piss and then stepped into the shower. Then suddenly, he thought about Shalon. He knew she would be calling him as she drove to work. She would always call around 8 or 8:30, but it was just past 9am and he had not gotten a single call from her all morning.

After Javoo got dressed he picked up his Blackberry and saw that he still had not gotten any calls. He quickly tried to call Shalon's number but she didn't answer, so he thought that he'd call Tracy to try to keep his plan in motion.

"Hello?" she said as she answered.

"Hi, cutie pie, how are you?" he asked her.

"Ok, I guess," Tracy responded.

"What's wrong sweetheart?" he asked, sensing something different about her tone.

"Nothin'," she said.

"Oh, I can tell that somethin' is wrong witcha because you don't sound too happy to hear from me," he said.

"Well, it's not you. It's just that me and Mitchell got into it last night, that's all," she told him.

"Y'all got into it, like how?" he asked.

"Really bad," she said.

"Bad, like hitting bad?" he asked.

"Yes, like hitting bad," she said back to him.

"C'mon, he didn't hit you, Girl," said Javoo.

"Yes he did, too," she said.

"For what Baby, damn?" he asked, sounding curious.

"He wanted to know where my girl Shalon lived for some reason," she told him.

"You talkin' about the girl you work with?" Javoo asked.

"Yeah, I tried to call her last night and this morning, but she didn't answer," Tracy said to him.

"Well, did you tell him where she lived?" he asked.

"He made me, hell, he was choking me," she told him. Javoo hung up the phone right in the middle of their conversation, rushed to get the keys to his black SS Impala and hit the door. He quickly drove down Martin Luther King Boulevard

146

and made a left to get on the freeway, as he called Cornelius's number.

"Yeah, what's up?" Cornelius answered still sounding sleepy.

"Get up man, I need you right now," Javoo said to him. Cornelius quickly sat up in his bed, while Chi-Chi lay still next to him.

"What's happenin'? You sound nervous," Cornelius asked him.

"It's Shalon, man. I think they got her," he told him.

"I'm at my apartment. Swing by here real quick," Cornelius said. Javoo had to go to Shalon's apartment. Something was telling him that she had been kidnapped and he wanted to see for himself.

"Naw, meet me at Shalon's apartment," Javoo said and then hung up. Cornelius hurried to his closet, threw on a Sean Jean warm-up, grabbed his gun and told Chi-Chi to stay there until he got back.

"What happened?" Chi-Chi tried to ask him, but he had already hit the door.

Javoo pulled into the parking lot of Shalon's apartment complex and parked. He could see that her car was still parked right in front of her apartment and wondered if she was still inside. His first thought was that maybe she had another nigga laid up with her, but then again, he had a key to her spot, so he didn't think she would do something as stupid as that. He sat there in his car for a few minutes and analyzed the surroundings, trying to see if he could find anything that looked suspicious, but everything seemed to be normal. There wasn't anybody standing around outside to ask any questions and he didn't wanna make it seem like he was trippin'. That's when he saw Cornelius turn into the parking lot and park. He knew he could always count on him when it came down to some street drama. He reached into his stash compartment, grabbed his 9mm, tucked it into his waist and got out.

"C'mon, let's go check it out," he said as he found Shalon's number on his phone and let it ring as they walked to her front door. They could hear her answering machine talking as he stuck his key in the lock and unlocked the door. The last thing they both wanted to see was Shalon lying dead on the floor when they walked in, but she was nowhere to be found. They began to look around in the apartment. It didn't look like she had been forced to leave or anything like that because Javoo knew that she woulda tried to put up a fight.

"Damn, they got her," he said, holding his head down. Cornelius looked at him.

"Hold up, we don't know that yet. She could be gone with somebody. Her purse is not here, and I don't see her car keys or her cell phone," Cornelius said to him.

Cornelius walked back out the door and over to the neighbors that lived to the left of Shalon and knocked on the door. He asked them if they had seen Shalon, but the girl and the guy living there both said no. Then he went to the girl's apartment to the right of Shalon's apartment, whom he had flirted with a couple of times, and knocked on the door.

"Hi, Diana," Cornelius said, once she opened the door.

"Um! Whatchu want?" she asked, thinking of the many times he'd promised to come over.

"You seen Shalon?" he asked her.

"Nope! I ain't seen her today," she said.

"Well, what about last night?" he asked.

"No, didn't see her last night either. All I saw was a black Tahoe parked next to her car. I thought she mighta had company or somethin'," she told him.

"Ok, thank you, Diana," he said and then walked back out to where Javoo was standing. Javoo leaned against his car, while Cornelius told him what Shalon's two neighbors had said. That's when he began to explain to him how Mitchell had jumped on Tracy and forced her to tell him where Shalon lived.

"You think the nigga still trippin' from that lick?" Cornelius asked him.

"Could be. But he coulda done this days ago," Javoo said as he continued to explain what he thought about Mitchell.

"I don't think he's really the type to just kidnap somebody, you know what I'm sayin'? He kinda went to the extreme to make Tracy tell him where Shalon lived. I'm willing to bet that Money Black made him do it," Javoo told him.

"But Money Black got plenty of bread. He don't give a damn about Mitchell gettin' robbed," Cornelius said to him.

"Yeah, that's what's fuckin' me up right now. Tracy told me that the nigga been playin' the tough guy role lately, and that was right after Chi-Chi's brother and his wife was found dead. He probably was there when they got killed," Javoo said to him.

"But still, what would make him just grab Shalon like that?" Cornelius asked.

"He probably didn't grab Shalon. Maybe Money Black's people did. I know he's probably trippin' behind the fires, so everybody is a suspect," Javoo told him.

"But why Shalon?" Cornelius asked him.

"I don't know. Maybe we got followed and he seen her. Maybe they think she got somethin' up with Smooth. It could be anything," said Javoo.

"You think the nigga know about us?" Cornelius asked.

"Maybe! I don't know what Shalon might say, so you start stayin' over at Chi-Chi's apartment, ok? Don't nobody know where she lives. Shalon doesn't know where I live either. She only knows your apartment. We also need to park these cars and get some more rentals. We can't afford to let 'em catch us slippin'," Javoo told him.

Cornelius knew that Javoo was totally upset, but the dude was extremely smart and his street sense was incredible. He knew Money Black had always had other people to do things for him. He wasn't as hands-on on the streets as Javoo was, and Cornelius felt like a war was brewing.

Chapter Seventeen

Shalon leaned against the pool table in Money Black's car and accessories shop. She had only a few days ago done a drive-by surveillance on the place, looking for a candy-blue Cadillac Escalade, and now she was standing inside the building with two of Money Black's men in the room with her.

"When y'all gon' let me go?" she asked, but they just stood there and said nothing. Suddenly, the door to the room opened.

"Damn you fine!" Money Black said as he walked in. He took a good look at her and then began to speak.

"I'm sorry for the inconvenience, lil mama, but I just had to see this 'Shalon' that everybody's been talkin' about," he said as he continued to eye-ball her from head to toe.

"Whatchu mean, everybody?" she asked.

"You know what I mean. Mitchell, Tracy, Chi-Chi, people like that," he said back to her. "And what did they say?" she asked him. "Well, they really didn't have to say anything. It's just kinda funny how you was with Mitchell when he was robbed, being that you work with his girl and all. I bet you knew everything about him before then, didn't you?"

"I don't know whatchu talkin' about," Shalon said to him.

"Ok, I'll go for that. But what's gettin' me is, now that I own Chi-Chi's brother's record label, you just so happen to be kickin' it with her, too," he said to Shalon.

"So! I can't have no friends?" she asked with a little sarcasm of her own.

"Oh, so she's yo' friend. Since when?" he asked. Shalon went on to tell him how it was a coincidence that she and Chi-Chi met. She told him that they met when the girl came to the mall to pick up something for her brother's wake and that's all it was.

"Who was them two niggas that robbed Mitchell?" he asked her.

"I don't know. They just came in pointin' their guns at me. Now can I leave? I been here all night," she said to him.

"Well, Mitchell told me that he locked the door, and his door wasn't kicked in, so that means you had to unlock it," he said, drilling her like an investigator. Shalon began to feel a little nervous. Money Black had thrown exactly what had happened right in her face and she never thought that she would end up in this situation.

"Well, I didn't unlock no door," she said as she started to walk towards the door of the room, but one of his boys grabbed her and pushed her back over to the pool table.

"Get yo' hands off me!" she said, swatting at the guy.

"Who's been settin' my shops on fire?" Money Black asked her.

"I don't know nothin' about no fires," she said.

"What's Chi-Chi up to? Did she hire somebody to fuck with me?" he quickly asked.

"I just met her. I don't know nothin' about none of her business ," said Shalon. The door to the room came open and in walked Mitchell. When she saw him, she thought that maybe he was gon' get Money Black to give her a break.

"Mitchell, will you tell him to let me go?" Shalon said, but Mitchell just looked at her. He had been fairly upset with her since he had got robbed and now she was standing there begging him to help her.

"Tracy know you doin' this?" Shalon asked him. Mitchell still didn't say a word.

Money Black continued to antagonize Shalon. He knew that she was guilty of something and he wanted to squeeze it out the best way he knew how.

"Take off your clothes," he said to her. Money Black was a cruel and treacherous man. His sarcasm would make a deadly situation seem to be not so bad, when in reality, it really was.

"Take off my clothes! For what?" Shalon asked.

"Cause I want you to. Now do you wanna take 'em off or do you want us to take 'em off for you?" he asked her. Shalon really didn't know what to do. She was starting to feel like she was in a no-win situation. "Come on. Let us have a look at that ass and that sexy body you got," Money Black said to her.

Shalon started to unbutton her shirt. She didn't want to get hurt or killed, and so she was gon' do what she had to until she could find a way to get out of there. She laid her shirt and bra on the pool table and quickly covered her breast with her arms. Her dark skin shined under the light that was beaming down on her. She was most definitely sexy.

"Take it all off," Money Black said as she stood there, like she hadn't taken off enough already. She began to unbutton her pants and then slid them slowly down her legs as she thought about Javoo. She hoped that he would come crashing in to save her, but she knew that wasn't going to happen.

"Girl, you shoulda been a stripper, damn!" Money Black said as he began to examine her body. He took Shalon's arm and slightly turned her when something real interesting came to his attention.

"Whoa! Come here, Mitchell," he called out. Mitchell walked over to where they were standing. "What do you think of this?" Money Black asked as he pointed at a small tattoo on Shalon's back.

Mitchell just shrugged his shoulders. "So what's this, lil' mama?" Money Black asked as he rubbed his hand over Shalon's tattoo.

"It's just a tattoo," she said. That's when Money Black looked at Mitchell.

"You know who this is?" he asked him. Mitchell shook his head from side to side, not recognizing the name that was tattooed on Shalon's back.

"Well, I know who this is," Money Black said, as he stood up on the pool table and walked back and forth, stepping all over Shalon's clothes.

"It's all startin' to make sense now. Mitchell, you got robbed and now my businesses is gettin' burned down. Take a look at that tattoo one more time. Anyone know who Javoo is?" Money Black asked, looking at Mitchell and then the other two guys. No one said a word and so he went on to tell them what he knew.

"Javoo is a jacker. The nigga is supposed to be a real beast on the streets. I done heard all kinds of stories about this fool hittin' licks. That's all he like to do. Nine times outta ten, bet he was the one that robbed you," Money Black said as he looked at Mitchell. Mitchell looked at Shalon and started to frown.

"Was it a tall dark-skinned nigga wit 'em when you saw 'em at the restaurant?" he asked Mitchell.

"Yeah," said Mitchell.

"Oh, he finally speaks," Money Black said as he jumped down from the pool table.

"Boy, I thought the cat had gotcha tongue," he said, reaching down to touch Shalon's pussy, but she only jerked away from him.

"If this nigga Javoo been hangin' around Chi-Chi, then he's the one that's been burnin down my shit. The nigga will do anything for a whole lotta money, and Chi-Chi got some dough" he said.

"He ain't burnin' down nothin'!" Shalon said, trying to defend Javoo. Money Black slapped Shalon back against the pool table. He had slapped her so hard that blood came from her lips.

"Bitch! Javoo don't do nothin' unless a lotta money is involved; I know it was him," he said furiously. He reached down and grabbed her arm to stand her up.

"Where the nigga live at?" he asked, and that's when Shalon spit blood in his face.

"You nasty bitch!" he said and then slapped her down to the floor once more. Shalon quickly tried to scramble away from him, but Money Black had told his two boys to grab her and hold her.

"Oh, you gon' tell me where the nigga live," he said as he reached into his pocket and pulled out a cigarette lighter. "Where he live!" he yelled, striking the lighter and putting the small flame to her nipple. Shalon wiggled and screamed.

"I don't know where he lives. He always come to my apartment," Shalon cried, as she watched the fire of the cigarette lighter.

"Where Chi-Chi live at?" he asked as tears continued to come from her eyes.

"I don't know. I told you I just met her, I don't know!" she said as Money Black put the lighter to her other nipple. Shalon wiggled and jerked with all her might, but the two guys that held her were just too strong.

"What's wrong? Don't you like to play with fire? Yo' nigga do," he said burning her nipple once more. Shalon screamed again. The pain was excruciating. She just couldn't take the heat coming from the small flame.

"Stop! Please stop!" she cried as Money Black burned her breast. Mitchell stood and watched as he tortured Shalon. He had known her for a while now, and never imagined he would see something like this happen to her.

"Mitchell! I want you to take this bitch somewhere down Highway 288. Find a nice long quiet road in a wooded area and ditch this bitch! Do her like you did Ralph," Money Black said as Shalon looked at him. Blood was still coming from her mouth and tears were still coming from her eyes. She sat naked on her knees, covering her breasts with her arms. She now knew exactly who it was that had killed Chi-Chi's brother Ralph, and began to think that she was about to be next. She just hoped that Javoo would come up with something to save her and fast.

Chapter Eighteen

Chi-Chi felt so terrible when Cornelius called and told her that Shalon had been kidnapped. She even felt so bad that she jumped in her car and raced over to Deno's house in 3rd Ward, just to see what they were going to do. When she got there, she could see just how upset Javoo was. In a sense, he was furious, but in another way, she could tell that he was hurt. She most certainly did not want something like this to happen. She had even come to the conclusion that if Shalon made it through this ok, then she would call off the whole thing about going up against Money Black. That's when Javoo told her that everything would continue to go as planned. Money Black had already made a big mistake when he killed Chi-Chi's brother, but to Javoo, he had made an even bigger mistake when he kidnapped Shalon.

Chi-Chi watched as Javoo jumped into the rental car and fired up the engine. Cornelius and Deno went to get in another rental parked behind his when Chi-Chi opened the back door and got in the car.

"Whatchu think you doin'?" Cornelius asked her.

"I'm goin' too, Cornelius, 'cause this is all my fault," Chi-Chi said, as her eyes began to fill with tears. Cornelius's phone began to ring. It was Javoo calling to ask what she was doing as well.

"Man, she say she's goin'," Cornelius told him.

"Ok then, tell her to come and ride with me," Javoo said and then hung up. Cornelius told her what Javoo had said, so she quickly got out of the car with them and went to get in with him.

"You gotcha cell phone witcha?" Javoo asked as he put the car in drive and headed for the freeway.

"Yeah, I got it," Chi-Chi said, fumbling through her purse nervously.

"I need you to call Smooth and have him to give you Money Black's number," he told her. Chi-Chi called Smooth right away. She was gon' do whatever she had to to help get Shalon back. She listened as the line buzzed and as soon as he answered, she got straight to the point.

"I need you to give me Money Black's phone number, right now," she said to him.

At this point and time, Smooth was down to do anything that she asked, especially after the way that Money Black had been treating him.

"You got it?" Smooth asked, after giving her the number.

"Yeah, I got it," she said, thanked him and then hung up.

Javoo had Chi-Chi dial up Money Black's number on his cell phone as he drove towards the Northside of town. He put the phone on speaker and listened as the line buzzed.

"What the business is?" Money Black answered, not recognizing the number.

"You the business Nigga," Javoo said to him.

"Who the hell is this?" asked Money Black.

"Nigga, you know who this is," Javoo said to him.

160

"Well, if it ain't Javoo! Damn Boy, how in the hell did you get my number?" Money Black asked, sounding surprised.

"I know the number to all the places my women be," he said, giving him a hint that he knew he had kidnapped Shalon.

"You gotta ho' at one of my spots? She must be a stripper?" Money Black said in an agitating way.

"Nigga, you know what I'm talkin ' about!" Javoo said, raising his voice over the phone.

"Nigga, do you know who you are talkin' to?" Money Black asked him.

"Right now, it really don't matter who I'm talkin' to, because the way I see it, it's a dead man on the other end of this line if I don't get Shalon back," Javoo told him.

"Shalon! Who the fuck is that?" Money Black asked him back.

"The person you scooped up in that bullshit ass black Tahoe you be ridin' in," said Javoo. Money Black knew that his SUV had been spotted. He told Mitchell and his two boys to hold up as they tied up Shalon. He didn't want them to leave with her and then get pulled over by the police, not knowing if anyone had reported his SUV or not. He knew everything would surely fall back on him then. That's when he began to think about Javoo and the money he had.

"How much money you willin' to drop for this bitch?" Money Black asked him. He thought that maybe he should try to negotiate with Javoo for Shalon. He knew he was as slick as they came and couldn't predict what might happen if something was to happen to her.

"I'm puttin' my whole life on it, Nigga," Javoo said to him.

"I mean money, Nigga. I ain't killed the bitch yet. I might fuck her though," he said, trying to aggravate Javoo.

"What kinda bread you talkin' about?" Javoo asked him.

"I'm sure you got some grip, after all the people you done robbed. Give me a mill, and I might let you get her back," Money Black told him.

Javoo pulled into a shopping center just down the street from Money Black's shop, as Cornelius and Deno pulled in and parked right next to him. He could see Mitchell's Mercedes parked out front next to Money Black's BMW and wondered just what was going on inside the place. At first, he thought about taking his gun and just barging into the place, but he didn't want to ruin everything that was going on for everybody else that surrounded him. Besides, he always did think that there was a better way of doing things, and Money Black was talking in his favor.

"Yeah, I think I can swing a mill, but you gotta give me until tomorrow to pull some of it out the bank," Javoo said to him.

"Tomorrow, huh? Ok then, call me at 3 o'clock sharp and have my fuckin' money, Nigga. I'll tell you what to do when you call," Money Black said and then hung up. Javoo knew that he had bought some time to deal with Money Black. He also knew that Shalon was still alive from the way that he spoke when he kept saying, "this bitch." Just from the sound of his voice, he knew she was right there in that car and accessories shop. He quickly called Cornelius' cell phone and told him to keep an eye on the place, while he and Chi-Chi made a quick run and for him to let him know if he saw anyone leave. His main concern was Money Black's black Tahoe. It had to be parked around back, he thought, as he looked at Chi-Chi.

She had noticed the candy-blue Cadillac Escalade as it sat out in front of the shop next to Money Black's BMW and Mitchell's Mercedes. Again, she thought about her brother Ralph and her sister-in-law Donna, as they sped away.

"I wish I could kill them motherfuckas!" she said, sounding very angry.

"Yeah, I feel the same way, Baby girl," Javoo said with his foot on the gas. They pulled up in front of a condominium complex out in the Alief area and parked. The sun was out and no one was around. That's when he reached into the back seat of the rental and picked up a Houston Astros ball cap. "Here, put this on," he said as Chi-Chi looked at him.

"What we fixin' to do?" she asked him.

"This is one of Money Black's spots. We gon ' check it out," he told her. Javoo knew the game. He knew that Money Black would never keep anything at his main spot, except for maybe a couple hundred grand. He knew street hustlers that sold lots of dope and handled lots of money, and each and everyone always had a condo, townhouse or just a regular apartment where they kept either drugs or money. It was what he did. Studying the streets was his M.O. and he knew the movements of almost every drug dealer, especially the ones that he was after.

"This gotta be it," he said, grabbing the large duffle bag that he took from Mitchell's condo. He explained to Chi-Chi that there shouldn't be an alarm to the condo. Money Black couldn't afford to have the cops walking all over the place in case someone was to accidently trip the alarm, and Javoo knew it. He remembered Smooth telling them that no one knew where he lived, so he couldn't have brought too many people over to that condo. His only hope was that no one was inside the place when he went in, and if they were, then God bless their soul.

"I'm gon' need you to stay close to me, ok, because I'm gon' have to kick the door in. Once we get inside, you check the kitchen cabinets, top and bottom, and all the closets downstairs.

I want you to even check the refrigerator. I'll check everything upstairs," he said as Chi-Chi fixed the ball cap snug on her head. Chi-Chi wasn't the type of person to break into someone's place. She had never done such a thing in her whole life and it made her wonder how breaking into Money Black's condo would free Shalon.

"We're lookin' for drugs or money, that's all, ok," Javoo said as they began to get out of the car. Chi-Chi looked down at what she was wearing. She wasn't dressed for this type of work, she thought.

"I shoulda wore my jogging suit, like I started to," she said looking at Javoo, as they both walked into the complex. She skipped along trying to keep up with Javoo as they walked down the sidewalk and turned into the gate that read number 5. When she saw him take out his gun, she didn't know what to think. Javoo took a quick look around and with no hesitation, he kicked the door in.

"C'mon," he said grabbing her by the arm, to help shake her nervousness. When they went in, they could see that no one was there. Chi-Chi ran to the first closet that she saw, while Javoo quickly fixed the broken door shut. He then turned and took the stairs two at a time, heading up to the bedrooms. It didn't take him no time to find the four large trash bags of money that Money Black had taken from Ralph's house. He grabbed two in one hand and two in the other, when he looked up on the shelf of the closet and saw 10 kilos of cocaine. He quickly grabbed them, threw them in the bags with the money and headed back downstairs where Chi-Chi stood with at least 300 ounces of crack she'd found hidden in the freezer and a few guns she had found stashed in one of the closets. Javoo quickly stopped to examine the guns. There was a Drug Enforcement Agent's .12-guage pump shotgun, a military issued M-5 assault rifle and a fully loaded AK-47. He hurried and took the large duffle bag from his shoulder and threw the guns inside it.

"Leave the crack!" he said as he threw the duffle bag with the guns in it over his shoulder and grabbed the trash bags full of money.

"Make sure you didn't leave any fingerprints anywhere," he told Chi-Chi. She quickly took the bottom of her shirt and began to wipe the edge of the kitchen counter and a couple door knobs. She wasn't takin' no chances on goin' to jail and was right behind Javoo when he walked out of the condo and went straight to the car.

"So what's in the bags?" she asked as she looked at him.

"Money," he told her.

"In all four bags? How much is it?" she asked as she looked in the back seat at the stuffed trash bags.

"I don't know. Maybe a mill or it can be just a few hundred thousand," he said back to her. Chi-Chi looked at the trash bags full of money once more and began to think about the time when she had walked into her brother's room, while he was counting money. He had counted nearly 2 million dollars and she watched him as he shoved the money inside 5 large, heavy duty trash bags.

Now she saw just how easy it was to get robbed. She had now become a robber herself and at this point, she would do anything she could to repay Money Black for everything he had done.

"I told him I was gon' give him a mill to get Shalon back, didn't I?" Javoo said, looking at her with a wicked smile of his own. Chi-Chi sat back with the thought of them giving Money Black back his own money for Shalon and smiled herself. It was exactly what he deserved. But if only she woulda known that that money had actually came from her brother's house, and that was something none of them would ever know.

Javoo picked up his cell phone and called Cornelius. He wondered if there had been any changes over at Money Black's car shop and wanted to do something quick, before he got nervous about holding Shalon and reneged on their deal. But Cornelius had told him that he didn't see anybody leave, except Mitchell. That's when he told him to meet them over at Chi-Chi's apartment, hung up and then made another call to Money Black.

"Yeah!" Money Black said as he answered.

"I gotcha money, Nigga," Javoo said to him.

"Damn boy, you work fast! Who you done robbed this time?" he asked him.

"You worry about that shit later, Nigga. Let's make a time to do this and get this over with," Javoo said to him. Money Black took a second to think. Not even a full 2 hours had passed and Javoo was already calling him with the ransom.

"Eight o'clock tonight, Greenspoint Mall parking lot, on the theater side, and don't be late," Money Black said and then hung up. He really had no intentions on handing Shalon over to Javoo. Like Ralph, he wanted to take him all the way out, and anybody else, if it came down to it.

Back at Chi-Chi's apartment, Javoo, Cornelius and Chi-Chi had spent several hours counting 1.5 million dollars in cash. Javoo figured that $500,000 would be justifiable enough as payment for all of them, considering the work they had to do to try to get Shalon back. They stuffed a million dollars back inside the large heavy duty trash bags and then checked the time. It was almost 7 o'clock and they had been waiting on Deno to go and steal an old hooptie from somewhere in his neighborhood. That was the car they was gon' use to transfer the money in.

"What about these guns and these bricks?" Cornelius asked Javoo.

"I'm gon' keep that for a coupla days. I gotta plan for Money Black and Mitchell's ass," Javoo said back to him and then looked at Chi-Chi.

"Chi-Chi, I'm gon' need you to report a breaking and entering, and a possible robbery at the condo we were just at,"

Javoo said as he pulled out a small piece of paper with the address to Money Black's condo on it. She stood looking surprised at what he was saying. She knew that they were the burglars and didn't want to make the call.

"Call the police! Whatchu want me to tell 'em?" she asked as she held her cell phone in her hand.

"Just tell 'em that you saw a coupla guys break into the condo. We gon' try to throw Money Black for a loop. Remember the crack we left," he told her. Chi-Chi stayed at the apartment and anonymously called and made the report, while Javoo and Cornelius went and met with Deno, who had stolen an old-school Cutlass Supreme from a dope-head that had been in the hood smoking crack all day. They put the money in the trunk of the Cutlass and headed for Greenspoint Mall. Javoo and Cornelius rode in two different rentals as they followed Deno. Javoo was in an all new Grand Marquis, while Cornelius drove a big Dodge Durango SUV, so they wouldn't get noticed.

When they got to the mall, Deno parked the car in the wide open so that Money Black could see the car. He got out of the old-school Cutlass, went and got in with his boy Cornelius and began to check his gun in case anything went down. Javoo parked on the other side of the parking lot and checked the military issued M-5 assault rifle he had taken from Money Black's condo. He was ready to get down to business, so he picked up his phone, called Money Black's number and waited for him to answer.

"You there?" Money Black asked as soon as he answered.

"Yeah, I'm here," said Javoo.

"You got the business?" Money Black asked.

"Oh yeah, I most definitely got the business. You got what I want?" Javoo asked him back.

"Yeah, I got whatcha want, Nigga," Money Black answered. Javoo knew that Money Black was gon' be deep with his goons. He knew that at least 3 cars would be following him, so he had to pretend to be just as deep. He could see the black Tahoe as it drove down the feeder and turned into the mall parking lot along with a few cars following it.

"Nigga, I know it was you who was burning down my businesses, and I know you was the one that got my boy Mitchell, too," Money Black said to him.

"Damn the small talk, Nigga. Let's get this over with before the parking lot security comes back around, and don't try no funny shit, 'cause I promise you, you will not leave this parking lot alive," Javoo said, sounding like a boss himself. Money Black took a look around the parking lot. His first thought was that of the police, but then he knew Javoo was a real criminal, so he couldn't see him having anything to do with the police, especially after all the shit he had done in the past. But still, he knew Javoo for being a serious individual, and he knew he wasn't going to back down.

"Ok, bring the money over to the black Tahoe," Money Black told Javoo.

"C'mon man, you think I'm stupid?" Javoo said back to him. Javoo knew that if he gave up his position, Money Black would have his boys to gun him down.

"Your money is in the trunk of that old-school Cutlass parked next to the street light. You see it?" he asked him.

"Yeah, I see it," said Money Black.

"The keys are in it, so have one of your boys go and confirm the business, and when he does, I want you to put Shalon out and tell her to walk to that black Dodge Durango," Javoo said to him. Money Black didn't want Shalon on his hands any longer. Even though he wanted to kill Javoo, he just couldn't risk going to war right there in the mall parking lot. He'd rather have the money just as well and deal with Javoo later.

Cornelius and Deno watched as one of Money Black's boys walked over to the car and popped the trunk. They were ready to gun him down if he tried to crank the car and leave without them seeing Shalon first. The door of the black Tahoe suddenly swung open and Shalon got out. She quickly walked over to the Durango, as the guy crunk up the old Cutlass and drove past her.

"Holla atcha, Lil' mama," the guy said and then laughed as he drove away. She had not had anything to eat and walked with a slight limp. Her face had been badly bruised and was purple from the abuse that Money Black had given her. Deno was thinking murder, as he got out, opened the back door and helped her in.

"I'll deal with you later, Nigga," Money Black said to Javoo, as he watched the Durango leave the parking lot with another car following behind it. Javoo wanted to know what kind of shape Shalon was in, so he quickly called Cornelius and asked him.

"Yeah, what's up?" Cornelius answered.

"How she look?" Javoo asked him, keeping an eye on the road and the other in his rear view mirror as they sped down 1-45 towards the south side of town.

"She don't look too good, my nig. She shakin' and all bruised up," Cornelius told him.

"Ask her if she needs to go to the hospital," he said. Cornelius passed Shalon the phone and as soon as she heard Javoo's voice, she began to cry.

"Do you need to go to the doctor?" he asked her.

"No, just take me home," she said to him.

"Not tonight. You goin' over to Chi-Chi's," Javoo said and then hung up. He knew that she couldn't live at that apartment any longer. He didn't want to give Money Black any other chances to catch her slippin', and once he found out that his money was missing, he knew that that was exactly what he might try to do.

Chi-Chi was already waiting in the parking garage when they pulled in. She could see Javoo as he got out and quickly walked over to the Durango where Shalon was. He immediately frowned at the sight of her face. She had her arms crossed in a sore-like position and her top lip was very swollen.

"Oh no!" Chi-Chi said, hugging one side of her as she helped Javoo walk her up to her apartment. They all sat around in Chi-Chi's living room and listened as Shalon told them everything Money Black had said to her. She told them everything he had done to her, but made sure they knew she stayed strong enough to make it through his torture. She told Javoo that she had not given him anything specific about him at all. Not because she could exactly stand the torture, but

171

because she simply couldn't tell him the things he wanted to know.

"I have to tell you somethin '," Shalon said as Chi-Chi handed her an ice-pack she had just made for her.

"What is it?" asked Chi-Chi.

"Mitchell was the one that killed your brother and his wife," Shalon said as she looked at her. Javoo and Cornelius looked at each other right away. "Money Black made him do it. They first kidnapped his wife, just as they did me, and then set it up so that your brother would have to come to them," Shalon said as tears began to fall from Chi-Chi's eyes. She thought, if only Ralph had been as smart as Javoo was. They suddenly thought about Tracy. She had to know what Mitchell had done and so they had Shalon to call her.

Chapter Nineteen

It was just past 9:30pm and all Tracy wanted to do was go home and relax in her Jacuzzi bath tub. She and another girl had worked all day, and had not taken any breaks, after Shalon had become a no-show. She wondered what was going on with her. Shalon had never done such a thing as not coming in to work or calling in. She had not mentioned anything about quitting and Tracy knew she woulda told her something if she was. She stuck the key into the ignition and crunk up her Murano. She was tired and the quietness of the mall's parking garage was making her even more sleepy when suddenly her phone began to ring.

"Hello," Tracy answered.

"Hey, it's me, Shalon," she said.

"Girl, where have you been? I have been tryin' to call you all day," said Tracy. Tracy was still wondering what Mitchell wanted with her. The light bruise on her face would not let her forget and now she was finally able to talk to her.

"Can you meet me right away?" Shalon asked her.

"Yes girl, where are you?" asked Tracy. "Well, I'm actually right here in the Galleria area, just a few blocks away from the mall," said Shalon.

"Ok, I'm leaving the mall now, so just tell me which way I need to go," said Tracy. Sensing that Shalon was about to tell her something about Mitchell, she began to frown at the thought of her sleeping with him. They had been friends for a long time and now this may be the end of their relationship, she thought. She also thought about the way Mitchell had been acting lately. She didn't know if it was because of Shalon or what. She just couldn't believe that he would play on her like that, if he did. She had a large amount of his money in her account, and plus he still had a key to her apartment, so she was hoping he wasn't trippin' like that.

"This can't be happenin," she said to herself as she pulled into the apartment building that Shalon directed her to, wondering why she was there. The thought of Mitchell paying for the place came into her head. Maybe Shalon was about to confess.

Javoo was waiting in the parking garage when Tracy pulled in. He had to break the news about playing her for the info she had given him about Mitchell and he thought that now would be the perfect time to do so.

"What's he doing here?" Tracy asked once she saw him. For the longest, she had always heard Shalon talk about Javoo, but she had never seen him to actually know who he really was. She only knew him as the kind fellow that walked into the store that she worked in and instantly swept her off her feet. "Hey, what's up?" she asked once she parked and got out.

"Hey, Tracy," he said back to her." My girl Shalon called me.

What's going on?" she asked him.

"Well, come with me and you'll see. We gotta lot to talk about," Javoo said as they walked towards the elevator.

"Where is Shalon?" asked Tracy.

"She's here, just follow me," he said leading the way out of the elevator once the doors came open. Tracy looked at him. He didn't appear to be the same as the days before. He didn't crack a smile or even attempt to hug her. She didn't know what the deal was, but it appeared that she was about to find out. That's when Javoo twisted the knob to Chi-Chi's apartment and showed her in.

"Oh, Girl!" Tracy said as soon as she saw Shalon. She quickly looked around at the people in the apartment and then went and sat next to her.

"What happened?" she asked Shalon.

"That's what we called you over to talk to you about," Javoo said to her. Tracy looked up at him and then again at everybody else.

"We know that you are probably wondering what this is all about, so I'll take it from the top," Javoo said and continued. "You see this girl right here? This is Chi-Chi. Her brother and his wife were just recently murdered," he said as Tracy looked at her.

"Ok, I think I remember her coming into the store," said Tracy.

"Well, the cops claim that they have no leads to the murders. A lot has happened since then and in the process, several people have come to her with a few details that led to a guy on the Northside named Money Black. That's who ya boy Mitchell gets his dope from," Javoo said as she continued to look at him.

"A little street work has led us to the conclusion that this guy Money Black orchestrated the murders, and we just found out that Mitchell was the one who pulled the trigger," Javoo said as Tracy gave him a strange look.

"Wait a minute! Are you telling me that Mitchell killed two people?" Tracy asked him and then looked around at everyone else.

"Well, when I talked to you at the clothing store, we were already on to Mitchell. That was my reason for meeting you like I did and I'm sorry about that. It was just something that I had to do to see if I could find out anything about him. After that, we did a few things to mess with this dude Money Black, and for some reason, he felt that Chi-Chi had somethin' to do with it, so he had Mitchell follow her," Javoo said and then began to question her.

"He does have a white Lincoln MKS with dark tinted windows and a black Mercedes Benz don't he?" he asked her.

"Yes," Tracy said as she slowly lowered her head.

"Well, Mitchell been tryin' to do some foul shit behind your back. I don't know if you knew anything about that or not, but Money Black ain't been makin' it no better. After we destroyed a couple of his businesses, he figured that since you and Shalon worked together, he could get Mitchell to make you tell him where she lived, especially after he saw Shalon and Chi-Chi together. That's why he wanted to know where Shalon lived so bad, and that's also why she looks like that right now," Javoo said to her. Tracy shook her head in disbelief. She couldn't believe what she was hearing.

"Did they kidnap you or something?" Tracy asked Shalon. Shalon nodded her head in sorrow.

"We just got her back tonight. I had to give this nigga a million dollars to get her back," Javoo told Tracy. Shalon looked up at him. She knew how he was about his money, but now she really knew that he cared for her, after giving up that kind of bread.

"They tried to make me tell them where he lived and where she lived," Shalon said, pointing at Javoo and then Chi-Chi.

"So, that's why he jumped on me last night. I didn't know what the hell was goin' on," said Tracy. Shalon went on to tell them how Mitchell just stood there and watched as Money Black slapped her around and then started to burn her breast with the flame of a cigarette lighter. That made Chi-Chi cover her mouth with her hands and Tracy's eyes get big, as tears began to come from Shalon's eyes.

"Tracy, you didn't know it, but Mitchell tried to holla at me behind your back. He ain't no good," Shalon said to her. Tracy and Shalon hugged each other. They had always had the utmost respect for one another and wasn't about to let someone like Money Black or Mitchell ruin their relationship.

"So who is this guy Money Black supposed to be?" asked Tracy.

"He a nigga with a few million dollars, who thinks he can do whatever he wants to people," Javoo said to her.

"Y'all shoulda called the police on his ass. Look what he done to my girl Shalon," Tracy said.

"He's got too much money to go to the police, being that we don't have a legitimate witness to testify against him for the murders," Javoo said.

"Yeah, he even forced the guy my brother left his record company to, to sell it to him by pouring gas all over him and threatening to burn him alive," Chi-Chi told Tracy. The whole world seemed to have closed in on Tracy. It was hard for her to believe any of this. She still had feelings for Mitchell and didn't want to believe he had done the things that they said he did.

"I have a lot of Mitchell's money in my account. Why would he jeopardize that or his freedom?" she asked.

"Well, evidently he didn't think about that when he jumped on you," Javoo said back to her.

"Yeah, you just might get to keep all that bread for yourself. That would be justifiable, considering the way he's been treating you lately," Cornelius said.

"So, what are you saying? Is something going to happen to Mitchell?" Tracy asked as she looked at him.

"You know, the way I see it, Mitchell is in trouble two ways. Either the police gon' get him for the murders, 'cause when it comes down to it, Money Black gon' make sure that happens, or he gon' die in the streets for tryin' to be slick," Cornelius said, feeling upset about what they had done to Shalon.

"Yeah, Mitchell is kinda in over his head, and there really ain't no way he can get out of it," Javoo said as he looked at Tracy.

"And I'm gon' see to it that they all pay for everything that they done," Chi-Chi said topping it off. Chi-Chi went on to tell Tracy about the type of money she had out on the table and the reason why Javoo and Cornelius were standing in her living room. After everything was said, it was Tracy's understanding that they were the ones that were going to take care of Money Black and Mitchell - not the cops. She started to feel like there was no way that she could turn her back on them, especially after everything she had just discovered.

"So what y'all think I should do?" Tracy asked them.

"Well, Shalon has got to move outta the apartment she live in. I can make that happen. I also think that you should move as well," Javoo told her. He explained to Tracy how Mitchell might come to her job to try to talk to her. He mentioned the fact that Shalon knew where she lived and where he lived, so by them kidnapping her, he probably would go into hiding for a few days, worried if Shalon would go to the police. That would give Javoo just enough time to call Stephanie and have her arrange some new locations for the both of them.

Shalon and Tracy both thought about the dramatic change in their lives all in just one night. Mitchell had become a very dangerous person under the spell of Money Black, but that was because he was just a natural flunky. They didn't want to get caught up in his deadly street scams and they sure as hell didn't want to cross paths with Money Black. That didn't rest the same in Javoo's book, though. He wanted Money Black just as bad as Money Black wanted him, but he needed to catch Mitchell first to make things right.

Chapter Twenty

Money Black woke up the next morning to the sound of his constantly ringing doorbell.

"Who the fuck is that?" he said climbing out of his king sized bed, where a naked dancer laid asleep. He looked at the TV monitors that the cameras around his house provided and saw a couple of Harris County Sheriff's Department cars parked out front.

"Damn!" he said, thinking that Shalon had gone to the police. He quickly went back over to the bed and snatched the covers off the naked dancer.

"Wake up, wake up!" he said as he shook her.

"I need you to go answer the door and tell the police I'm not here. Tell 'em I went out of town," he said as the doorbell continued to ring. He had the million dollars Javoo had given him in his closet and couldn't afford to let the cops find it.

"C'mon now, hurry up," he clapped his hands and said.

"Ok, ok," the girl said as she threw on one of his robes and headed downstairs. She could see two uniformed officers through the glass standing at the door.

"Yes, can I help you?" she opened the door and asked.

"We're looking for a Mr. Eric Dywane Williams," one of the cops said.

"Well, he's not in at the moment, he's out of town," said the girl.

"We want to report a burglary at a condominium that's registered in his name, at 2727 Hathaway Drive, apartment number 5. We want to ask him a couple of questions," the cop said to her.

"Well, like I said, he's out of town," the girl said. The officer dug into his pocket, pulled out a card that had a constable's name on it and gave it to her.

"Could you have him call this number when he gets in?" the officer asked her. The girl nodded her head and looked at the card as she slowly closed the door. She didn't want to have nothin' to do with no police and so she looked back through the glass once again and watched as they got back into their cars and left.

"What did they say?" Money Black asked as she walked slowly back upstairs.

"They said somethin' about an apartment that got broke into, that's in your name or somethin'," she said as she yawned and laid back across the bed.

"Whatchu mean apartment? What else did they say?" he asked.

"They said the address is 27 somethin'. I can't remember. All I know is that they said apartment number 5," she told him. Money Black thought about the trash bags full of money and the kilos and guns he had in his condo.

"Here, they said that they want to ask you a coupla questions," the girl said as she handed him the card the cop had gave her.

182

"What the fuck is goin' on?" he said to himself. He had been hit real hard in just one week. First, two of his businesses had been burned to the ground and now a burglary at his condo. He just knew his money and his dope was gone. He all of a sudden thought about Javoo.

"Nah! The nigga don't know nothin' about that spot," he said in a low tone. He went to his closet and opened one of the large duffle bags to see if he could recognize any of the bills, but it was just too much money to tell. He figured that no one knew where he kept his drugs and, most of the time, he would hardly stash both money and drugs in the same place. But somebody had caught him slippin' while he held Shalon hostage.

"I knew I shoulda smoked that bitch," he said as he lit up a cigarette and turned to the girl lying in his bed. "Get up, baby, we gotta go," he said to her. He had to go check out his spot. He thought long and hard on who coulda broken into his condo, but Javoo just kept popping up in his head every time. He knew that that's what he was good at - hittin' major licks. He had heard about him too many times. The guy had become such a legend that even some of the rap artists in the studio that had never seen him or knew who he really was, would rap about him in their music.

"Bitch-ass nigga!" Money Black said as he pulled up in front of the condominium complex and parked. He took a look around and then slowly got out. Everything seemed to be normal to him as he walked into the gate and up to the front door. He could see a shoe print still on the door where some-one had kicked it in.

"Damn!" he said and then stuck his key in the lock, twisted it and turned the door knob. He noticed as he entered that the frame around the door was crooked and weak from the blast of the kick. Straight upstairs he went and, just like he figured, the money and the kilos were gone. He quickly went back downstairs to the kitchen and looked in the freezer. All of the ounces of crack were gone as well. That's when he thought about the guns and walked over to the closet and opened it. They were also missing. He shook his head from side to side trying to control the rage that was brewing inside, when he noticed that something was different about the kitchen. His microwaves were gone.

"Now what motherfucka would steal a nigga's micro-waves?" he said, talking to himself.

Money Black had three microwaves he had bought at a Walmart just a few blocks away and had been using them to cook up crack with. Now they were missing, along with everything else that he had in the condo and he thought that was really strange.

He left the condo and headed for his car and accessories shop when he got a call from Smooth.

"Yeah, what's up?" he said as he answered.

"Say, we have to post-pone Young Thug's album until next month because he has some new tracks he wants to add to it, and we have to change the order of a few songs," Smooth told him.

"Ok, but next month, we droppin' that boy work," Money Black said back to him and then hung up. It seemed like every corner he turned became a dead end. He had no way of finding out the things he wanted to know and his small group of goons were useless when it came to detail. No one knew Javoo's real name and Chi-Chi had suddenly moved. She was using other people to run her businesses just to stay on the low, and now he was thinking about burning them down just to get even.

The only thing that was making him think twice about that was she was too legit and had too much money for a legal dispute. He knew he had been arrested before and had even been under an investigation for moving dope and hoggin' people, and she had people like Shalon on her side who could testify against him about his illegal activities.

He wanted to just book a flight and leave town, but something told him not to. The game and the life in the streets had surrounded him. He had once thought about going all the way legit with his business, but the fast life and the money that came along with it was just too lovely, and it seemed that he had been swallowed completely whole.

Money Black noticed a tinted, unmarked car get in traffic behind him as he turned onto the street of his car shop. The cops had already been to his home earlier that morning, so he thought nothing of the unmarked car until it turned into the parking lot of his car shop behind him.

"What this motherfucka want?" he said, as a man in civilian clothes, wearing a pair of sunshades, met him at his car.

"Mr. Williams!" the man said as Money Black got out.

"I'm Detective Rollins from the Harris County Sheriff 's Department. I visited your condo late yesterday evening. Seems like you had a break-in," the detective said to him.

"A break-in?" Money Black said, as if he was unaware of what he was talking about.

"Yeah, could you tell me who occupied that condo?" he asked him. Money Black couldn't quite figure out what to say. He had been caught by surprise by the man and he knew he was about to be thoroughly questioned.

"A friend of mine," he responded.

"Could you give me his name?" the detective asked, looking at him over the top of his shades.

"Well, what's the problem?" Money Black asked him.

"When we got the report that there was a break-in and a possible robbery, we took it that there could be a possible home invasion and responded to the call. We could tell that the door had been busted. Once we went inside, it appeared that no one put up a struggle or a fight, so we knew it wasn't a robbery. But what we did find was about 300 ounces of crack, sitting on the kitchen counter. Now, could you explain that sir?" the detective asked, giving him the whole scoop. Money Black was even more surprised. He'd thought that whoever had broken into his condo had taken the crack. He didn't know that it was left for the cops to find.

"Crack! Whatchu mean crack?" asked Money Black.

"Now come on, Mr. Williams, we could tell that the condo was being used as a manufacturing spot, and you mean to tell me you knew nothing of this?" asked the detective sarcastically.

"No, not at all," said Money Black.

"Ok, just give me the name of the person that occupied that condo. We just want to ask him a few questions," the detective said to him. "He mails me his payments, so I don't know what's goin' on," Money Black said as he pleaded his innocence.

"So what's his name then?" the detective asked.

Money Black was stuck between a rock and a hard spot. He didn't know what to say or whose name to use, but he had to think of something and fast.

"His name is Mitchell. Mitchell Simmons," he told the man. Mitchell was the only person that he could think of outside anyone else that hung around on the Northside. He knew that the man didn't know who Mitchell was and doubted that the detective would end up just bumping into him. He also knew that if he didn't give the man a name, he would end up arresting him, and so he felt content with the name that he gave him.

The detective took a small notebook out of his pocket and wrote down the name that Money Black gave him.

"Ok, Mr. Williams, you might want to go check that out," the detective said as he turned and walked back towards his car.

Money Black began to walk to the front door of his car shop and just as he grabbed the door handle, he heard the detective call out to him.

"Oh, one more thing, Mr. Williams! Tell him that we'll send those microwaves back when we get through testing them for prints and drug residue. See you around," the detective said as he smiled and got back into his car and left. Money Black felt a little edgy. He knew no one had been using those microwaves but him, but still, he wasn't tryin' to hear nothing about going to jail. Now the cops may come back to arrest him for sure. He had been robbed, paid back his own money for Shalon, and set up for the police. He was really beginning to think that it was all being done by the one person that needed to be taken off the face of the earth: Javoo.

Chapter Twenty-one

Javoo called up Stephanie early the next morning. He had already talked to Chi-Chi about taking Shalon out to meet her and had asked her to act as if she was just trying to help a friend who had been battered by her boyfriend and was trying to get away from him. Tracy's situation was a little different and a lot easier. Her credibility to purchase a new pad was all the way up to par, especially with the type of money she had in her account, so Stephanie was more than pleased to do business with her.

He knew he had to make things right for Shalon. She had been through too much and in too short a period of time. She had, in the last week and a half, participated in a robbery, been duct taped and left to free her own self, and then had done a surveillance job on the very same people who had kidnapped and tortured her. He had given Chi-Chi a large portion of the money they had taken from Money Black's condo in exchange for the check she was gon' give Stephanie for Shalon, just to keep business straight.

"Hey, hello Javoo," Stephanie said as she answered.

"I need you again," Javoo said to her.

"Ok, whatcha got?" she asked him.

"I got some real good business for you this time, but you gon' have to cut me a deal," he told her.

"Cut you a deal huh? You must have some really good business for me then," she said.

"I got two girls and both of 'em need new places. They have the money and the class for a nice location. One already has a sky rise apartment near downtown and the other is just lookin' to upgrade after having a situation," Javoo said, putting the steam in Stephanie.

"I think I can swing that, but I'll have to check on a few things first, ok? So I'll call you back," she said ending their conversation. Javoo didn't get in until around 2:30am, once Shalon had fallen asleep at Chi-Chi's. He had had a long day the day before and just being able to lie in bed for an extra hour that morning was making him feel a whole lot better. His wife Tanasia had even made him breakfast in bed before she left for work, to make up for giving him such a hard time once he did finally come in. He had brought in another bag of money, which was his excuse for staying out so late, and the only thing she could do was just accept his explanation.

Javoo laid in bed and thought about his boy Cornelius, wondering what he was up to. He and Chi-Chi both had been highly upset about what had happened to Shalon, and her agreeing to help both Shalon, and Tracy was no problem considering what she had learned about Money Black and Mitchell.

"Let me call my boy," he said as he reached over to the nightstand to pick up his cell phone. He quickly found Cornelius' number and waited for him to answer.

"I was just about to call you," Cornelius said as soon as he answered.

"What's the deal?" Javoo asked him.

"Man, it's Chi-Chi. She trippin'. She didn't sleep at all last night. We gotta do somethin', my nig," Cornelius said to him.

"What's wrong with her?" asked Javoo.

"It's Mitchell. She trippin' on how this nigga came to her and everything," he said.

"Put her on the phone," Javoo said after hearing her cursing in the background. He could hear her voice get louder as she came near the phone.

"Man, this nigga got me fucked up, Javoo! He killed my brother. I wanna do him myself," Chi-Chi said as she breathed heavily over the phone.

"Calm down Chi-Chi. I'm working on it right now," Javoo told her.

"I'm for real man! And then he gon' let this nigga do this shit to Shalon, after he had known her for so long," she said, still breathing heavy.

"Where is Shalon, Chi-Chi?" Javoo asked her.

"She in the bathroom."

"Ok, tell her I'll be over in about 30 minutes. In the meantime, I'm gon' need you to call Smooth and ask him if he could tell you anything," he said to her. Chi-Chi hung up the phone and called Smooth right away. He told her that Money Black seemed nervous about something, but couldn't tell exactly what it was about, so he told her he would try and find out and would let her know once he did.

Javoo knew that something had to be done but first, he had to make sure that those girls were safe. He fired up the engine of the Grand Marquis and headed towards Chi-Chi's apartment as he thought about how all the pieces had fallen into place. He had given Chi-Chi just over $100,000 to see business through with Stephanie, but she ended up giving most of it to Cornelius and he was cool with that. It wasn't just about the money to her, and he knew it. She got off on the way that he handled his business against Money Black. It made her feel good to know that he was getting everything he deserved, and with a million dollars on the table, Javoo was gon ' make sure he did.

He also thought about Shalon's well-being. He had planned on giving her $150,000, courtesy of Money Black, once she got situated in her new spot. He had also kept a large portion of the money for himself, in case everything they were trying to do fell through.

Once he made it to the apartment building he tapped on the door of Chi-Chi's apartment. He hated what had happened to Shalon and was glad to see that she was feeling a lot better. Shalon was sitting on the couch looking at her face in a small mirror. Her face was still bruised, but that didn't stop her from still wearing a nice looking outfit that they had rounded up from her apartment during the course of the night.

"You ok?" Javoo asked as he sat down next to her and kissed her on the cheek. Shalon nodded her head. She was glad to see him. She had never met anyone like him, and even though he was married to another woman, she was down with him to the end.

"You ready to do this?" he asked her about going to check out her new place. Javoo began to explain to Shalon how she and Chi-Chi were going to meet Stephanie once she called and told him she had found a spot for her. That made her start to feel grateful for what they were doing. The money that they threw around was like winning the lottery to her. She had never seen anyone make the kind of moves that they did and with that amount of money. He had told her that he was gon' fatten up her bank account so that she could live comfortably in her new place and for her not to worry. That's when his cell phone suddenly started to ring. It was Stephanie. "What's up, Steph?" he asked as he answered.

"Ok, I've got two great locations for you," she said as Javoo listened.

"One is in the Memorial District. It's a nifty little loft, for sale by the owner, at $90,000. It's a 2 bedroom, 2 bath, 2 story, with a balcony on the top floor - a great place," she told him.

"Is it in the building where the roof top party was?" he asked her.

"Yes, I forgot about that," she said and then continued. "Anyway, the other one is in Imperial Valley, $1,800 dollars monthly, or it can be purchased for a $170,000. It's a large condo, 3 bedrooms, 2 bath. It also has a 2-car garage, a Jacuzzi, and comes with a really nice view. The homeowners association provides residential security patrols and, of course, the place has its own alarm system. She'll love it," Stephanie told him. Javoo told her that Chi-Chi and Shalon were going to meet up with her. She gave him the address and the directions to both places and then they hung up. Next they called Tracy, told her what was going on and for her to have everything she needed to purchase the condo when she went to go meet Stephanie. He also asked her if Mitchell had called, but she said that she had not heard a word from him, which was a good sign for the time being.

"Are you ok?" Javoo asked Tracy.

"Yeah, I'm ok. Just a little confused about everything that's happening. I still can't believe it," she said, sounding sluggish on the phone.

"Well, it's true," he said to her. Tracy had finally realized that Ladarian Walker was really the guy Shalon had spoken of all along. She even realized that Shalon knew that he had been gettin' at her too. But once Javoo broke it all down to her, she totally understood and decided to just be down with his game plan.

"Ok, you call me if Mitchell calls you today," Javoo said to her and then hung up. Chi-Chi and Shalon took the Dodge Durango that Cornelius had rented out to meet with Stephanie, while he rode with Javoo in the Grand Marquis. They had to figure out how they were going to get Money Black and Mitchell. As they drove down the freeway trying to put their plan together, Cornelius' phone began to ring. It was Chi-Chi on the line.

"What's up Baby?" he said as he answered.

"Smooth just called me saying that he talked to Money Black. He said that Money Black told him that the police questioned him about a break-in at his condo. Tell Javoo they found the dope," Chi-Chi said, sounding excited. Javoo smiled once they hung up. That was exactly what he wanted to happen. Now Money Black would have to stay on the low. It also meant that Mitchell wasn't going to be able to purchase any drugs from him and would soon come out of hiding and start looking for Tracy. Once he did, they were going to be waiting for him.

Chi-Chi and Shalon rode towards Memorial as they began to talk. They had hardly known each other and Chi-Chi thought that now would be a good time to get to know her.

"So how long have you been seeing Javoo?" she asked Shalon.

"Almost a year," Shalon responded.

"You must really love him?" Chi-Chi asked as she looked at her face.

"Yeah, I do," said Shalon.

"Well, he really is something," said Chi-Chi.

"What about you and Cornelius?" Shalon asked her back.

"Me and Cornelius used to go together a while back, but I stopped seeing him when him and Javoo took some money from my brother. A coupla years had passed and when my brother was killed, I went to look for him. So I guess I never stopped loving him either," Chi-Chi said as she looked at her again.

"Well, you know we can all get caught up in our feelings," Shalon said, as they saw Stephanie's car parked at the loft building.

Cornelius wondered where Javoo was heading as they took the I-10 freeway from the 610 loop. They had been talking about Money Black and Mitchell, and he wanted all of this to be over just as bad as Chi-Chi did. Javoo first told him that he wanted to set it up, so that both Money Black and Mitchell could be in the same place at the same time, but once he thought about Tracy, he figured that it would be better if they caught Mitchell all by himself. He thought that maybe Mitchell would spill the beans on Money Black then for sure.

"We're goin' out towards Money Black's house," Javoo said to Cornelius.

"You think he'll be there?" Cornelius asked, feeling for his 9mm.

"I doubt it. He ain't gon ' rest, being that a lot of his money came up missin'. Plus, the cops have already questioned him about that work, so nine times out of ten, he'll stay away from his house as much as he can, in case they come to arrest him. He might even be out lookin' for us right now," Javoo said as Cornelius looked at him.

"You think we can get that nigga Mitchell though?" he asked.

"Oh yeah! That ain't no problem. As long as Tracy has his money, we can get him," Javoo replied. Javoo went on to tell Cornelius how he planned to use Tracy to get Mitchell, but he still had to find out how he was gon' get Money Black away from the rest of his goons. He knew he didn't care too much for women, so he couldn't get him that way, and he definitely couldn't just call and tell him to come and meet him again either. That was completely out of the question. That's when the thought of Stephanie and her ability to find new places struck him and he picked up his cell phone to give her a call.

"Yeees Javoo!" Stephanie answered, as if she'd been interrupted.

"Did the girls make it?" he asked her.

"Yes, we're at the loft building now," she told him.

"Hey, what have you and your girlfriends been up to lately?"

"Just working," she said to him.

"I think we need to have another one of those casual drinks and maybe listen to a little music this time. Besides, you been such a big help, I could kiss you myself," he said as Stephanie giggled.

"You know, as a matter of fact, we're due for a good time. It's been a couple of weeks since we hung out anyways," she said to him.

"Ok, you call me when your business is done and we'll meet up," Javoo told her and then hung up. He wanted to get a good look at Money Black's crib, just to see if he could possibly get into the place and to see if Mitchell could be hiding out there as well. He turned down the street that Money Black lived on. A small waterfall stood at the entrance of the neighborhood as they drove into the gated community. They could see the automatic sprinklers watering several lawns. There were tall walls covered with ivy surrounding some of the homes, while a few of the other homes had tall gates with their family's name adorning the entrance to their driveways.

They came up on Money Black's house and slowly drove by. His house was a smooth looking 2 story with at least 5 bedrooms. He didn't have a gate out around the front of his home, like a lot of the other houses, but he did have a tall wooden fence that covered the entire back area, where you could tell he had a swimming pool and a garage big enough to hold at least 6 cars. There were also cameras on each of the corners of the house, and Javoo could see a Brink's Home Security sign sitting out on the lawn as they drove by.

"I just wanted to check the nigga out," he said, really admiring Money Black's taste.

"I know you ain't thinkin ' about runnin ' up in the nigga house, is you?" Cornelius asked him.

"Nah, it's too risky. Plus I gotta better idea," he said as Cornelius continued to gaze at some of the other houses they were passing and headed back to the freeway.

Chapter Twenty-two

Mitchell had stayed the previous two nights at another one of his girlfriend's house. He didn't wanna be nowhere to be found if Shalon would have went to the cops for what Money Black had done to her. He was thinking that she shoulda told Tracy about everything by now. She had not called him and he was starting to wonder what was on her mind. Their relationship over the past few days was on the rocks, but then seemed to be just a bad spell that had been casted upon the both of them. He knew she was in love with him and figured that after a few days had passed, she would be worried and start calling him, but he still had not heard a word from her. He finally made it back to his apartment, parked his Lincoln and then hopped back into his Mercedes, hoping that he could get her to talk to him.

"I gotta go by her job," he mumbled, after he tried to call her but got no answer.

It wasn't like her not to answer his call. Usually, if she was mad at him, she would still answer. But just with a nasty attitude. Then he thought about how he had treated her, slapping her down to the floor and calling her a bitch while he stood over her. He then called Money Black's number, thinking that it would help get Tracy off his mind.

"Yo' what's happenin'?" Money Black said answering the call.

"You tell me," Mitchell said back to him.

"Aw, man! Shit's gettin' deep," said Money Black.

"Tell me about it," said Mitchell. Money Black didn't want to tell Mitchell that some money had been taken from him.

"Somebody broke into one of my spots yesterday and now the cops is fuckin' with me about some work they found," he told Mitchell.

"You think it was that Javoo nigga?" he asked him.

"I don't know, maybe. I'm still tryin' to figure it all out myself. But hey, I'm gon' have to talk to you about that later. Until then, we gon' have to hold up on that business for a few more days, because I don't know if the police will be watchin' me or what," Money Black told him.

"Ok, just hit me up when everything is cool," Mitchell said and then hung up. Mitchell barely had enough drugs to supply some of his customers, but at least it was something he could do until this shit about Shalon blew over. He had already made a decent amount of cash over the past few days, especially since he and Tracy had not been getting along, and he was thinking that now was a good time to try and make up with her.

He parked his car in the valet section of the mall and went in. As he passed the Cheesecake Factory, he thought of the many times he and Tracy would go and have lunch there. The mall was at its usual stage and people were busy walking throughout the place, dipping in and out of stores, just as they would always do. He came up on the store where Tracy worked and went in.

"Hello!" Mitchell said to the girl that was working there.

"Oh, hey, Mitchell, how can I help you?" she asked him.

"Is Tracy here today?" he asked as he looked towards the back of the store.

"No, she hasn't come in yet," said the girl.

"Do you know what time she's comin' in?" he asked.

The girl looked Mitchell up and down. She knew he often came to the store to pick up Tracy and take her to lunch, but something told her that if he didn't know where she was, then she didn't want him to know.

"You know, I don't know if she's even comin' in at all today - her or Shalon," the girl said back to him.

"Ok then, thank you," he said and left the store. The first thing Mitchell could think of was that Shalon might have told her everything. But he still felt like she woulda called him, even if it was just to curse him out. He pulled out his cell phone and called her number again, but still got no answer.

He knew he still had a key to her apartment, but he was too scared to go there, especially after what he had done and then seeing Money Black torture Shalon. He didn't know if Tracy had called the police on him for hitting her or what. He didn't know what to think. Suddenly, something that was real important to him came into his head. The thought of all the money he had in her account was forcing him to have to go by her apartment.

Mitchell unlocked the door to Tracy's apartment and walked in. "Where this bitch at?" he said to himself as he

201

looked around. He checked the caller I.D. to see what kind of calls she had gotten. None from the Houston Police Department, which was a relief to him. He then tried to call her from her own home phone. Still no answer. Something just didn't seem right. Two nights had passed since he last saw her, and it was quite understandable why she wouldn't answer. He had hit her. He started to think about the night she came in drunk, and then another night when she came in late. Maybe she was creepin' with somebody else, he thought. He thought of so many things that could possibly be going on, but his main concern was his money, so he had to talk to her and soon.

* * *

Tracy met with Stephanie, Chi-Chi and Shalon over in Imperial Valley. Shalon had already told her everything about her new place and now Tracy was checkin' out hers.

"This is very nice. Very roomy," Tracy said to Stephanie, as she pictured how she wanted the place set up.

"So you like it, huh? Well, it's yours. All you gotta do is just say the word," Stephanie said as she looked at Tracy. Tracy looked back at Shalon and Chi-Chi, then shrugged her shoulders.

"Go on and take it," Chi-Chi told her.

"Yeah, switch up, Tracy, I have," said Shalon.

"Ok, ok, I'll take it," Tracy said as they stood by the kitchen and made the arrangements. She had put her phone on vibrate, but still noticed every call Mitchell had made to her. She thought if everything that Javoo told her about him was true, then it will all soon come to light. But then she began to think, if it wasn't, she would really have some explaining to do about why she spent that amount of his money on the condo. She had been only renting the place that she lived in, which was really taxing her to the fullest. She had to work long hours and even sometimes on her off days just to maintain her life-style, but now, she owned this place. She would only have to pay her yearly taxes on the property and the utilities that came along with the place and she figured she could handle that.

"Ok, everything is set," Stephanie said to Tracy and then shook her hand. Chi-Chi and Shalon both hugged Tracy, congratulating her on getting her new place. They arranged it so the same moving company that had moved Chi-Chi would move Shalon and Tracy, but Tracy was still just a little nervous about something.

"Girl, Mitchell's been calling me all morning," she told Shalon and Chi-Chi, once Stephanie had left.

"Let him keep calling," said Shalon.

"Yeah, girl, you gotta get away from him first," Chi-Chi told her.

"But he called me from my apartment. He has a key," Tra-cy said, still feeling nervous. Tracy didn't want him to be there when the movers got there. She knew he would be highly upset if he found out she was trying to move on him without telling him first. He had already jumped on her once and she definitely didn't want him to jump on her again.

"Let me call Javoo and Cornelius and see what they want us to do," Chi-Chi said as she took out her cell phone and called Cornelius. Cornelius told Javoo that Mitchell had been calling Tracy all morning and that the girls were stuck on what to do. That's when he told him to tell them to go back to Chi-Chi's apartment and to stay put until they got there.

* * *

Thanks to Javoo, Stephanie had made two profitable sales for the day and it was only just past 2 o'clock in the afternoon. Her name would surely be placed on a trophy plaque as Sales Person of the Month at the real estate company she worked for. Business had been tough until she met him. He had given her a boost, just as he had done his boy Cornelius in the past. Mostly everyone in his immediate circle had come up on something. It wasn't always just about him, and Stephanie was smart enough to recognize that. She pulled out her cell phone and called her friend Marissa, the girl that worked for U.S. Customs out at the airport.

"Yeees, darling!" Marissa answered in a sexy tone of voice, like she would always do when they joked with each other.

"Hey girl, what are you doing?" Stephanie asked her.

"I'm heading home. My day is over, thank God," Marissa said, sounding relieved to be off duty.

"You sound like you had a rough day," said Stephanie.

"Yes girl, I did. The airport was crazy today. Thought we had a terrorist boarding a flight. Turns out, he was just an Iranian doctor trying to get back to New York. We had to hold the flights for five and a half hours before any of the planes could leave," she told her.

"Well, it sounds like you need a drink," said Stephanie.

"I could use a bottle," joked Marissa.

"Our friend Mr. Javoo is inviting us to a casual evening, if you are up for it," Stephanie said to her.

"I'm always up for partying, you know that," said Marissa.

"Fine, then, I'll call Laura and we'll meet him and Cornelius for happy hour," Stephanie said and then hung up. Next she called her friend Laura and gave her the details. Laura, who was a flight attendant, had been on vacation for nearly two weeks and still had one more week to go before it was time for her to go back to work. She felt like she had already run out of things to do, so going out for happy hour was right up her alley.

After Stephanie finished talking to Laura, she called Javoo and told him that they would meet him and Cornelius. But even after she talked to him, she began to think about the girl that she sold the loft to. Her face had been badly bruised and she wanted to ask Javoo what had happened to her. Stephanie thought that Shalon seemed to be such a nice girl. She had managed to get the loft down to $75,000, as a part of the deal she had promised Javoo. How could she have refused him? He was the one and only reason why an additional $50,000 had been placed in her account for the commission of sales, after selling those places to Chi-Chi, Shalon and Tracy.

But everything was still a mystery to her. She was wondering how he persuaded those women to buy the places that they did. She thought, either this guy had to of had a helluva conversation, or he was just someone who happened to just hang around a bunch of high-priced women. But how could he get three people to just up and move like that, and in an instant? She could tell from the small amount of time that she spent with the girls that their decisions to move were made overnight. Then she thought about the Maserati she saw him in when they first met. She even remembered seeing him leave the rooftop party in a white Mercedes Benz.

"A person that owns a day care couldn't possibly afford those types of vehicles. What are you up to, Mr. Javoo?" she mumbled to herself.

He had not tried to sleep with any of them. Her half-black, half-Vietnamese look made her hard to resist. She knew she had an incredible figure and exotic looks, which was part of the reason why she had made the sales she did long before she met him. She thought, "How could he ignore a woman like her?" Her beauty, her body and her intelligence had her quite confused as to why he had not noticed her, and she was now interested in finding out what he was all about.

Chapter Twenty-three

Javoo and Cornelius met Chi-Chi, Shalon and Tracy back at Chi-Chi's apartment after they had stopped by his house to switch back into the Range Rover.

"You girls like your new spots?" Javoo asked as he threw his arms around Shalon.

"Yes, I do," Shalon said as she looked up at him with her bruised face. She really wanted to thank him for what they had done, but they were trying to figure out what they were going to do with Mitchell.

"What about you, Tracy?" he asked her.

"It's a very nice place. I'll have to get used to it," she said.

"Ok, now y'all gon' have to lay low, just for a coupla days," he told them.

"But what about Mitchell? I have to go to my job this evening and work until closing time. I know he gon' come up there," Tracy told him.

"Don't worry about that, ok? If he calls you, tell him to meet you in the parking garage. We gon' grab him, so don't trip and start doin' all that loud ass screamin', ok? Just get in your ride and follow us. Do you understand?" Javoo asked her.

Tracy nodded. She had never been involved in these kind of activities and now Javoo was asking her to sit back and watch the guy she loved be kidnapped.

He then turned to Chi-Chi and told her that he wanted her and Shalon to be there as well. He had a few tricks up his sleeve and one was the plot he had to get Money Black. He knew Stephanie could be persuaded into playing an important role for him and so he had to get to that club to talk to her. He talked to Shalon for a few more minutes, gave her a hug and a kiss, then he and Cornelius left for Club Grooves.

Stephanie, Marissa and Laura were already in the parking lot waiting when Javoo and Cornelius pulled in. Cornelius noticed that they were all sitting in Stephanie's black 4-door Volvo as they pulled up behind them and blew the horn. That's when they all got out and walked over to where Javoo parked.

"So, you have a Range Rover, too?" Stephanie said as she gave Javoo a tight hug.

"Yes, I do. Are you not surprised?" he asked with his usual flyness, while he hugged the other girls.

"You know, I have to thank you for turning me on to those girls who bought those places," Stephanie said.

"Me? Turnin' you on? WOW! I might get lucky tonight," Javoo said as Stephanie hit him on the arm while the other girls giggled. Javoo paid the way in for everyone as they all went to the bar and got their favorite drinks. He needed to talk to Stephanie and was noticing that she was watching every move he made. She eyeballed him even when a couple of guys came over to shake his hand and spoke to him and Cornelius. She watched everything. She noticed how he didn't speak to no one, but was always spoken to. She even noticed how he had gotten the doorman to let them skip the small line of people outside the club and allowed them to go straight in.

"C'mon, let's grab that booth," Javoo said as he saw a group of women leave a booth they'd been sitting in. The order that they sat in made him and Cornelius look like two of the most playa-made men in H-town, with Marissa sitting on the outside, then Javoo, then Stephanie, then Cornelius and then Laura. Everybody in the club seemed to be looking their way. Cornelius continued to whisper in Laura's ear, while Javoo spoke with Stephanie and Marissa. Marissa was telling them about the scare out at the airport when the waitress brought over a tray loaded with drinks. They had ordered two drinks for each of them. Marissa had already downed the drink she had when they first got there and was halfway thru her second when Blame It On The Alcohol by Jamie Foxx and T-Pain started playing.

"Ohhhhhh! That's my song!" Marissa and Laura both screamed.

"C'mon Cornelius," they both said, pulling him from the booth to go and dance with them. Javoo just shrugged his shoulders after Cornelius looked at him like he needed help. He wasn't much of a dancer at all and so Cornelius was on his own.

"So, Mr. Javoo, what's your story?" Stephanie asked him as she sipped her drink thru a straw, looking at him intensely.

"What story are you talkin' about?" he asked her back.

"Well, you bump into us at a restaurant one lovely afternoon and you tell me that you own a daycare. But then I see you in all these fancy cars and, to top it off, you have three people purchase around three hundred thousand dollars worth of lofts and condos," she said to him.

209

Javoo knew exactly what Stephanie was getting at. She wanted to know about him and what he really did for a living.

"So what are you asking me, Steph? You think I'm a drug dealer or somethin'?" he asked her.

"Are you?" she asked.

Javoo smiled. "No, I'm not," he answered.

"Look, man, you can be straight up with me. I haven't been honest all my life either," she told him. Javoo took a deep breath. He really didn't meet with Stephanie to give his life story, but he had to somehow get her to understand what kind of person he really was.

"Well, Steph, these days you gotta be bona fide on the streets, genuine. I grew up on the streets. I came up as a thug, hustlin' and robbin' people. Nobody gave me nothin'. My parents were druggies, dope fiends and alcoholics, so I had to live with my grandmother. It was tough for me as a kid. Once I learned that money meant everything to me, I decided that I would find a way to get it, no matter what steps I had to take to get it, or the extremes I had to go to," he said as she looked at him.

"Well, what about those girls?" she asked.

"Shalon, Chi-Chi and Tracy are three sweethearts. I met them all in a time of need and I helped them," he said.

"Tell me about Shalon," she said.

"She's a girl that I been seein' for nearly a year. I met her at a club," he told her.

"So, did you do that to her face?" Stephanie asked him.

"Hell naw! I wouldn't do that to a female, but I'll tell you what really happened if you promise me you can keep a secret," he said to her. Stephanie nodded her head yes.

"Shalon was kidnapped. I had to pay a guy a million dollars to get her back. That's why I had her to move out of her old place," he said as Stephanie gave him a surprised look.

"Are you serious?" Stephanie asked him.

"Yeah, I'm serious. You remember when I had you call and ask your lawyer friend for the name of the guy that owned the record company of the guy that was killed?" Javoo asked Stephanie.

"Yeah, you mean the Williams guy," she said.

"Well, that's the same guy who kidnapped Shalon and we think he's also the same guy that killed Chi-Chi's brother just a couple of weeks ago," he told her. Stephanie looked at Javoo with an even more surprised look. The things he had told her were deep; deeper than she had ever imagined.

"Did anybody call the cops?" she asked him.

"Well, no one can put this guy on the scene of any of these things, except Shalon, and this guy has too much money. He'll either get off or get a light punishment for kidnappin' her, two years, maybe five. Chi-Chi has offered me a lotta money to find out if this guy murdered her brother and I have done that. But the problem is, we both know each other, him and I, and it's kinda hard for me to get close to him. He even made one of his boys jump on Tracy, just to find out where Shalon lived. He's outta control," Javoo said and then took another sip of his drink.

"We gotta do something! We can't just let him get away with this," Stephanie said, which was exactly what Javoo wanted to hear.

"We? Whatchu mean, we? This is somethin' I gotta handle. This dude kinda made it personal, you know?" he said, looking more serious than ever.

"Look, if you need my help on anything, you know you can count on me, right? Stephanie asked.

"You know, as a matter of fact, I do need your help on somethin'," Javoo said. Javoo continued to tell Stephanie everything that he knew about Money Black. He even mentioned the time that they had gotten into a fight. He told her that he needed her to find a place so that he and Money Black could meet and that he was gon' need her to give him a call when the time was right. He'd even told her about Smooth and how he ended up in the position that he was in.

"So, you think he kidnapped Shalon just to get back at you?" she asked him.

"No, he really call his self tryin' to find out why she and Chi-Chi were hangin' out together and what Chi-Chi was planning. I had destroyed a couple of his businesses and he thought Chi-Chi mighta had somethin' to do with it, so I guess they thought Shalon knew. He mistakenly saw my name tattooed on Shalon's back and that's when it became personal," Javoo told her.

Stephanie put her hand to her head. She could now feel the pain that Chi-Chi and Shalon felt. Now she understood why they had to purchase those apartments.

Cornelius, Laura and Marissa came back to the table after they finished dancing. They had worked up a sweat, along with an appetite, and ordered up a few appetizers.

"Ahhh! This is what I needed," Marissa said as she leaned back in the booth.

"Yeah, thank you for a lovely evening," Laura said as she smiled at Javoo.

Javoo looked at Stephanie. He knew that she was feeling everything he had told her. He also knew that he could trust her and the other girls, too, but for now, she was all he was going to need. He had told her that he was gon' need her to play the role of a big time representative from Colossal Records and for her to call Money Black and tell him that she needed to meet with him and Smooth to discuss some promotional business, and Stephanie had the perfect place to make that happen.

Javoo checked his watch and noticed the time. He and Cornelius had to get back and switch cars once again. He didn't want to miss Mitchell in case he went by Tracy's job. He wanted to be there.

"Ok ladies, we gotta roll," Javoo said as he and Cornelius stood up and started hugging the girls.

"You be sure to call me," Stephanie told him as they walked towards the exit of the club. "I'll call you first thing in the morning," Javoo said and then walked to his Range Rover.

Chapter Twenty-four

Mitchell drove his Mercedes slowly through the light near the Galleria Mall as he checked his watch once again. He knew that Tracy would be getting off work any minute and he did not want to miss her. He turned into the parking lot and drove his car towards the parking garage. There he could see her Nissan Murano parked next to a black Dodge Durango, as he drove on by and parked in an empty space just two cars over. He knew he had a lot of making up to do with her, and he figured that this would be his best chance to see her and talk things through. He picked up his phone and called to see if she was coming out.

"Hello?" answered Tracy.

"Are you about to get off work?" Mitchell asked her.

"Yes, I'm walking out the door now," she said.

"Why haven't you been answering any of my calls?" he asked.

"Because."

"Because of what?" he asked her back.

"You act like you haven't done anything," she said to him. Mitchell sat silently on the phone for a second. He didn't know if she was referring to what happened to Shalon or what.

"That's why I want to talk to you," he said.

"Well, we can talk about this later," said Tracy. "C'mon, baby! I'm in the parking lot waiting on you," he said to her.

"Whatever!" Tracy said and then hung up. Her heart started to beat fast. If Javoo was going to do what he said he was gon' do, then Mitchell was in for a big surprise, she thought. She quickly found his number and called to see if they were there.

"I already see him," Javoo said as soon as he answered.

"Just walk to your ride like you normally do and don't forget to follow us," he told her and then hung up. Mitchell could see Tracy as she walked past a few cars. He stepped out of his car and walked over to where her Murano was parked and waited.

"Hi, baby," he said as he attempted to kiss Tracy when she walked up, but she just turned her head away. She was still highly upset with him from the night that he jumped on her, not to mention everything else she had learned about him.

"C'mon, baby, don't act like that," he said grabbing her by the arm. Tracy looked down at his hand, reminding him of the night he hit her.

"Act like what? Like I told you on the phone, you act like you haven't done anything. Who do you think you are?" Tracy asked as she reached for the door to her Murano. Mitchell stood in front of the door. He wasn't about to let her leave without talking to him first. Suddenly, the doors to the black Durango flew open and that's when Javoo, Cornelius and Deno jumped out with their guns pointed at him.

"What the fuck!" was all Mitchell could say before Javoo cracked him over the head with the butt of his pistol.

"Deno, grab his keys and follow us. You too, Tracy," Javoo said as he and Cornelius picked Mitchell up and quickly threw him in the Durango. Javoo jumped in the back seat with Mitchell, while Cornelius got in the driver's seat, fired up the engine and drove away. They had some business to take care of with Mitchell and when they saw Chi-Chi and Shalon heading their way, Cornelius quickly called and told them to turn around and follow. They drove over to 3rd Ward, where Deno had an old shack he had converted into a sort of club-house. The place looked like a meeting place for thugs and carried a dungeon-like look on the inside.

"Take him and chain him up," Deno said as the girls all parked out front and got out. Mitchell was still out cold. Javoo and Cornelius put him in a steel chair Deno had personally designed, and with the chains locked down tight on him, they were sure to find out everything they wanted to know.

"Wake up, Playboy," Javoo said, tapping Mitchell on the side of his face with the palm of his hand.

"Awwwww!" he moaned as his eyes slowly came open.

"Bet you didn't figure this was gon' happen, did you?" Javoo asked as he stood in front of him. Mitchell's head was still spinning from the blow that Javoo had given him.

"Who is you? What y'all want?" he asked.

"We want you to tell us what you know, that's who we is," Javoo said to him.

"Whatchu talkin' bout?" Mitchell asked as he slowly came to.

217

"We talkin' bout you bein' a bad boy lately. We been watchin' every move you make," Javoo told him.

"I ain't done nothin' to nobody," he said.

"Oh, you and Money Black, y'all been doin' some ratchet-ass shit out here in these streets, boy," Javoo said. Mitchell raised up his head. He could finally recognize Javoo and Cornelius from the time he saw them at the restaurant with Shalon and Chi-Chi.

"You told Money Black about Shalon and then y'all kidnapped her. And what was so bad about that was you just stood there and watched him torture her," Javoo said as he continued to grill him.

"Now this the same girl that's friends with your girl Tracy, and this the same girl that you tried to holla at behind your girl's back. I wonder what Tracy woulda thought about that," Javoo said to him.

"Nigga, you don't know whatchu talkin' bout," Mitchell said, growing angry.

"Oh, I think I do know what I'm talkin' bout, Killa. See, how would I even know that Tracy was your girl, and how would I know that you jumped on her to find out where Shalon lived if I didn't know what I was talkin' about? You coulda just asked her where Shalon lived; you didn't have to beat her up. That's where you fucked up at," Javoo said as Mitchell grew even madder.

"Tracy don't run shit, Nigga. I do," Mitchell said as he pulled at the chains that were clamped down tight on him. "But ain't this the same girl that you let keep your money?" Javoo asked as Mitchell gave him a surprised look.

"Tracy my bitch! She do what I tell her, Nigga," he said, not knowing that she was standing right behind the chair that he was sitting in. Javoo knew he had struck a nerve in Mitchell. Everything he was saying to him was on point and Mitchell was getting uptight.

"That's just part of it, nigga. See, you one of those dudes that wanna be a G-Nigga, when you really just a flunky for Money Black," Javoo told him. Mitchell spit at him. He didn't like the way that Javoo was labeling him.

"Nigga, you don't know whatchu talkin' bout," Mitchell said as he pulled at the chains once more.

"So, you tellin' me that Money Black didn't send you by the house of the girl whose brother you had just killed?" Javoo asked him. Shalon walked over to where Javoo was standing and when Mitchell saw her, his eyes got big.

"I heard Money Black tell you to do me like you done Ralph," she said as she looked at him. Mitchell was in a situation that he couldn't get out of. Shalon was a number-one witness to everything he had done, and he knew he couldn't beat around the bush any longer.

"Yeah, but the nigga made me do it," he said. Right away, Chi-Chi ran over and started hitting and scratching him all in his face.

"You sorry, punk-ass, bitch-made Nigga!" Chi-Chi screamed as Cornelius came and pulled her away from him. Mitchell started to plead for his life. There stood the girl he took part in kidnapping, and another whose brother he had murdered.

"It was all Money Black, I'm tellin' you. He set up everything," Mitchell said as he started to cry like a baby. Tracy walked around the chair and stood in front of him.

"I can't believe you!" she said and then slapped him as hard as she could. It stunned him to see Tracy in the old shack with these people. He didn't think she would ever turn on him. Ever!

"Baby! Please, baby, just listen to me," he said, looking at her and then over at Javoo. "I can fix this," Mitchell said.

"How you gon' do that? You already killed this girl's brother. You already jumped on Tracy and you already helped them kidnap Shalon," Javoo said to him.

"I can set Money Black up. I can bring him to you," Mitchell said, still crying.

"Listen to you. You sound like a snitch-ass motherfucka," Javoo said as he walked over to the door and opened it. "Shalon, you and Tracy go home," he told them. Tracy took one more look at Mitchell and then spit in his face.

"I hope you go to hell," she said and then walked out the door, with Shalon following her. Javoo picked up the M-5 assault rifle that was leaning against the wall. He had taken the gun from Money Black's condo and figured that now would be a good time to use it. That's when he looked over at Chi-Chi. He could see tears still coming from her eyes but this time, it wasn't from feeling hurt about what had happened to her brother. It was from the anger that surged through her veins.

"Let her go, Cornelius," Javoo said to him. Chi-Chi walked over to where Javoo was standing. He grabbed her by the hand and put the gun in her palms.

"C'mon, man! Please don't do this," Mitchell cried as Chi-Chi looked at him.

"Did you show my brother any pity when you murdered him and his wife?" she asked him.

"Look at me, Nigga!" she shouted as he began to lower his head. Chi-Chi pointed the gun at him. She began to tremble as her brother's face flashed in her head.

"When you see my brother, I hope he kill yo' ass again," she said and then squeezed off three rounds into Mitchell's chest. Chi-Chi dropped the gun, ran over to Cornelius and buried her face in his chest. As Mitchell's body slumped over in the steel chair, she cried hard and loud, finally able to release the pain she felt when her brother was killed.

"Get her to the house, Cornelius. Me and Deno will take care of this," Javoo told him. Deno had two boxes of large heavy-duty trash bags. They quickly put on a pair of gloves, wrapped Mitchell's body in the trash bags and then duct taped him from head to toe.

"We gotta dump this nigga," said Javoo.

"I know where we can take him," said Deno. Javoo drove Mitchell's Mercedes with his body in it, while Deno drove the Durango. They drove over to McGregor Park in Southpark, parked the car and then set it on fire.

"C'mon, we gotta make a quick stop," Javoo said as he put Mitchell's key to his condo in his pocket and got back into the Durango.

He thought about Chi-Chi and wondered how she must be feeling. That's when he picked up his phone and gave Cornelius a call.

"What's up?" Cornelius answered. He had driven Chi-Chi's Corvette while she sat on the passenger side in a daze. He knew she had never used a gun, especially one to commit murder.

"Everybody ok?" Javoo asked him.

"Yeah, everything cool," Cornelius said back to him.

"Ok, you stay there with her and I'll see you later," Javoo said to him and then hung up. Javoo had to go to Mitchell's condo one more time. He knew that Mitchell had not been keeping any money or drugs at Tracy's since he had jumped on her, and he wasn't able to deal with Money Black at the moment, so he had to have something stashed somewhere.

"Where we headed?" Deno asked Javoo.

"We goin' to get some money, my nig," Javoo said to him as they cruised down Old Spanish Trail. It was just past 11 o'clock pm and Javoo thought that the time to go by Mitchell's condo was perfect. He pulled up at the visitor's parking space he and Cornelius had parked at before and got out.

"This the spot," Javoo said as he tried the first key to Mitchell's condo, then the second. The lock to the door clicked and they went in. Deno knew the routine. He had hit a few licks in his time also, and didn't push the candy-red Cadillac that sat in his driveway from just selling dope. He quickly checked all the closets downstairs, the bathroom and the kitchen, while Javoo quickly checked upstairs. But Javoo knew exactly where to look and immediately went to Mitchell's bedroom closet. There he found another duffle bag full of money.

"Stupid ass nigga," he said, grabbing the bag. He looked and saw a kilo of cocaine sitting in a shoebox next to a pair of Michael Jordan tennis shoes. He knew Deno woulda wanted the brick, so he threw it in the duffle bag and headed back downstairs where Deno stood with a pound of marijuana he had found stashed in Mitchell's refrigerator.

"Let's go," Javoo said as he shoved the weed in the duffle bag and forced the zipper shut. So far, everything he had planned was on point. Now all he had to do was count that money and split it up, which was payment enough for a full day's work.

Chapter Twenty-five

Tracy dropped Shalon off at her new apartment and went on home. She had a helluva lot of decorating to do, she thought as she walked in. The moving company had moved all her things in, but had placed most of it in the garage and in the living room.

"Ah, what a mess," she said once she walked in. Boxes and furniture were everywhere. She even had to put her own bed back together after the moving company just sat the mattresses and headboards in her bedroom. As she put her bed together she began to think about Mitchell and seeing him chained to the steel chair. They had been dating for a while and now she realized that he had been doing nothing but using her as a stash for his business.

"I wonder what they are going to do with him?" she asked herself. She knew that he would soon come to look for her, especially behind the money. She had moved on him without saying a word and he had seen her with all the same people that Money Black despised the most.

That's when she began to feel scared. She had to know what Javoo had done with him. She went to her purse, dug out her cell phone and called Shalon. Shalon was already in the decorating mood. She too had to sort through all of her stuff and had started to hang up clothes and putting other things into her bedroom. She was very much wide awake and had finally gone into the bathroom to look in the mirror at her bruised face.

"Mitchell had finally met his match," was all she could think of. She began to smile at the thought of seeing him crying and begging Tracy as they both walked out the door of Deno's dungeon.

"That's what his ass get!" she said as she raised up her shirt to look at the bruised burns on her breasts. The funny noise of her cell phone ringer sounded and she hurried to answer it, hoping it was Javoo calling her, but it was Tracy.

"Hey, what's up?" Shalon asked as she answered.

"Girl, I'm trying to figure all this shit out. These people got my stuff everywhere," Tracy said to her.

"Yeah, I know. They did me the same way," Shalon said.

"Hey, whatchu think they did with Mitchell?" Tracy asked her.

"I don't know. I'm still waiting for Javoo to call me," Shalon told her.

"You know, after the things he did and said, I really shouldn't care, but it's been bugging me to know," said Tracy.

They both wanted to say that Mitchell might be dead, but neither one of 'em could come up with enough strength to spit it out. They weren't the type of women to bear witness to a murder and just sit back like it was something they did on a regular basis, but Javoo had made them leave and now all they could do was wonder.

* * *

Cornelius sat at Chi-Chi's dining room table and watched as she walked back and forth from the bedroom to the living room and back to the bedroom over and over again. He could see that her nerves had gotten the best of her and she just could not be still. She had even formed some kind of a code of silence and hadn't said a single word since she pulled the trigger on Mitchell. She was beautiful and rich, he thought as he continued to look at her, but with the guts to kill to go along with it. He knew she was all the way in now. He stood up and reached for her as she attempted to walk past him again.

"Hey, hey, Baby. How do you feel?" he asked her.

"I'm ok, I guess," she said back to him.

"Are you sure? Because you keep on walkin' back and forth like a zombie," he said jokingly. Chi-Chi cracked a short smile. "Yeah, now that's what I'm talkin' bout Baby. That's better," he said as he hugged her.

"Now I know. I finally know everything that happened to my brother and Donna," Chi-Chi said as she turned and walked away from him with her hands on her hips.

"Yeah, now all we gotta do is get Money Black and all this shit is over," Cornelius said, as if they had been on a long journey.

"So, how we gon' get him?" Chi-Chi asked.

"I think Javoo got somethin' set up for tomorrow, but I don't know exactly how he plans to do it," he said to her. They talked for a few more minutes when suddenly they heard a knock at the door. Cornelius took out his gun, went and looked through the peep hole and opened the door, once he saw it was Javoo.

"Boy, I thought I was gon' have to bust somebody in their ass," he said after Javoo saw the .9mm in his hand. Javoo walked right over to Chi-Chi and gave her a light hug.

"You ok?" he asked her.

"Yeah, she is ok, just a little nervous that's all. I just stopped her from walking a hole in the floor," Cornelius told him. Javoo knew exactly what he meant. It had stuck in his head, seeing the way that Chi-Chi held the gun in her hand when she pulled the trigger on Mitchell. It was like she had done it a thousand times already.

"Tomorrow, we gon' get Money Black, ok?" Javoo said as he looked at both of them. He had come through like never before for Chi-Chi. Now she knew that she could trust him. She just hoped that his plan against Money Black would be just as devastating as Mitchell's was.

"Here you go, homey," Javoo said as he flipped Cornelius a bag with something inside it.

"What's this?" he asked after seeing the money inside the bag.

"It's your part of what me and Deno took from Mitchell's spot. It's 50 G5," he said as Cornelius reached over and gave him some dap.

"I gave Deno 50, so everybody shoulda came up on somethin' tonight. Chi-Chi got the information she needed and the actual guy that killed big bro, and Tracy gets to keep all the money Mitchell had in her account for herself. Now all I gotta do is hook Shalon up with some bread and we straight," Javoo said, nodding his head in a satisfying way.

"So what about Money Black?" Chi-Chi asked Javoo.

"I need you to call Smooth and tell him that somebody gon' call him and Money Black with some special details. Tell him it's going to pertain to the record company and for them to follow the instructions the woman is going to give him. Also tell him to make sure he talk to Money Black about it so he won't think that somethin' fishy is goin' down. Y'all both be ready in the morning, ok?" he said to them. He reached into his pocket, pulled out a bag of weed and tossed it to Cornelius.

"Here, this is for you," he said and then walked out the door.

Chapter Twenty-six

Money Black woke up the next morning feeling better than the days that had passed. The owner of the local strip club that he normally went to told him that he had planned on selling the place and since he came in all the time and spent a lot of money, he thought that he'd give him first chance at purchasing the place, since all the girls already knew him.

"Can't stop me," he mumbled as he thought about what had happened to the clothing store and the beauty and barber salon. He reached over, picked up the remote to his TV and pressed the power-on button.

"Last night, a body was found inside a burning vehicle in south Houston. Authorities are investigating the murder," the news woman went on to say as Money Black got up and went to go brush his teeth.

"Damn, somebody got fucked off again," he said, still listening to the news from the bathroom. He then began to think about Smooth. Smooth had called him late last night and told him about the meeting they were supposed to have with the Colossal Records representative. He hadn't ever met with any big time business people before and he wanted to look his best. He went to his closet, opened the door and pulled out one of his most expensive suits.

"Ha ha! Business as usual, you bitch," he said as he thought about Chi-Chi. Money Black laid a red power tie and some sparkling cuff links next to an all-black suit. Colossal Records had given Ralph a $20 million dollar deal and he had promised to uphold the deal after taking over the company.

"Smooth, yo' ho 'ass might as well get ready to drive," he said as he picked up his phone to call him.

"Wud up, Black?" Smooth said as soon as he answered.

"I'm comin' to pick you up. You gon' drive, ok?" Money Black told him.

"That's cool. I'll be at the studio and we'll leave from there," Smooth said as he heard a sudden click from Money Black's phone.

"Rude ass nigga," Smooth said to himself, thinking of what was going to happen. He thought about the scam that Javoo had created and he hoped that it would work. It had to. There was no way Money Black would let any of 'em rest if it didn't.

Money Black had bought a 2-toned Maybach several months ago and hadn't ridden in it but twice. Now that he was about to go and meet with some big time business people, he wanted to make it look good by making Smooth drive while he lounged around in the back seat. He went over to the TV monitors that showed all sides of his home, thinking to himself how he was gon' take care of his business with the record company people and then find a way to get back at Javoo. He had went too far burning down his businesses, and he wanted to really make him pay. As a matter of fact he was more than sure that was gon' happen, but business was business and, for now, Javoo was in the clear.

* * *

Javoo woke up early with Tanasia and the kids. He had come in quite early as far as Tanasia was concerned. She was always used to him coming in around 3 or 4am, but 1:30am was much better and she felt like she had gotten a full night in bed with him. He helped dress the kids for school while she whipped up some bacon and eggs quickly before they had to go. He had promised her that he was gon' start spending more time around the house, and she thought that maybe he was coming down with something and went to touch his forehead with the back of her hand.

"You alright?" she asked him.

"Yeah, I'm alright," he said, knocking her hand away from his face.

"I'm just tryin' to see if you ok. You talkin' bout spendin' more time around the house and all. Hell, if it wasn't for me and Javon, them damn dogs would starve to death back there. It would be a miracle to see you hang around here anyways," she said as she gathered up the kids and left for work.

"She don't know what she talkin' bout," he said with his jaws full of the bacon and egg sandwich she had made for him. He grabbed his phone and called up Stephanie.

"Hello, Javoo," she said, nearly answering his call on the first ring.

"Damn, you fast," he said.

"Well you said you needed my help, so I was waiting for your call," she said to him.

"Oh, ok then, what's the deal?" he asked her.

"Tell me what you need and I will try and find it," she said.

"I need you to find a place that's empty. I need it to be a classy looking place but with no people around and then I'm gon' need you to call the guy I told you about and make sure he understands that you're a big time Colossal Records representative," he told her.

"So you need him to come to this place, right?" she asked.

"Yeah," said Javoo.

"You know we can't be having no shooting and all that wild shit at these kinda places, don't you?" she said to him.

"Trust me, it won't be nothin' like that," he said back to her.

"Ok, let me check through my map sheet and see what I can come up with. I'll call you when I'm ready," said Stephanie.

"Hey, don't worry, you'll be taken care of," Javoo said to her and then they both hung up.

Javoo and Deno had taken $275,000 from Mitchell's condo. He had already given him and Cornelius $50,000 each and was going to give Stephanie $25,000 just to keep her honest. He had taken another $50,000 for himself and was going to give Shalon $100,000 to set things straight with her as well.

Next, he called Cornelius and Chi -Chi and told them that he was going to come over to sit with them while he waited for Stephanie to call. He wanted to already be at the place when Money Black got there. He picked up the large duffle bag with the 10 kilos and the guns in it and put it in the back seat of his Range Rover. At first, he was wanting to fuck him off, just as he had done Mitchell, but since Stephanie was going to be there, he had conjured up a much better plan.

"You had a nice run, nigga," Javoo said to himself as he drove his Range down the 610 freeway heading towards Chi-Chi's apartment. Suddenly, his phone began to ring. It was Stephanie calling.

"What's the deal?'·' he asked as he answered.

"Ok, I've gotta place out in Clear Lake," she continued to tell him.

"It's a mini-mansion that's been renovated into offices on the inside. It used to be a huge law firm. The address is 605 Clearwater Drive. I'm headed out that way now," she told Javoo.

"Did you make the call? he asked her.

"Oh yeah, he fell for it," she told him.

"Ok, Stephanie, that's some good work. Now I need you to call this guy Smooth and give him the address. Tell him to be there at 11 o'clock this morning," he said to her. Stephanie hung up and immediately called Smooth, while Javoo swung by Chi-Chi's apartment and then headed out to Memorial to pick up Shalon. He just felt like it would make her feel a whole lot better if she were there to watch Money Black go down.

Javoo noticed the curtains being pulled together in Shalon's loft as they drove up. She came down and stepped out of the front door, wearing her fashionable attire as usual. She wore a Louis Vuitton sun cap, belt and sandals, over a pair of

Christian Dior shirt and pants. Her face was still bruised from what Money Black had done to her, but she had not lost her fashion sense.

"Hey, y'all," she said as she got in the front seat of the Range Rover. Everyone was stone faced and looked like they were ready for war, she thought, as Javoo put his ride in reverse and headed out towards Clear Lake. He explained in detail everything he wanted done once Money Black got there. He wanted to make sure everyone understood their position. He had told Chi-Chi to call Smooth and see if he was ready, but Smooth was already on top of everything. He too was ready to get this over with. He hated being told what to do by Money Black and now he was thinking it was time for him to get what he right fully deserved.

* * *

Money Black listened to a copy of Young Thug's album as he pulled up to the studio. He blew the horn, got out and then slid into the back seat as he waited for Smooth to come out.

"Brang ya ass on, Nigga," he said as he saw the silver and yellow tie of Smooth's suit come closer to the tinted glass door of the studio and then again as he walked out to the car.

"Man! This a throwed ride," Smooth said as he sat in the driver's seat and looked back at Money Black.

"So who you think you suppose to be, Sean "P-Diddy" Combs?" Smooth asked with a fake smile on his face.

"Yeah, and you Fonzworth Bentley," Money Black said as he gave him a sly grin. Smooth put on his seat belt and then put the car in drive.

"You know how to get there?" Money Black asked him. "Yeah, I got the address and the directions in my pocket. We gotta go out to Clear Lake," Smooth told him.

"Ok then, let's ride," Money Black said after seeing the briefcase Smooth had put on the floorboard on the passenger side.

"So what's in the briefcase, Terrance?" he asked him.

"It's some of our paperwork, just in case they wanna see how we manage some of our artists," Smooth said as Money Black nodded his head in a satisfying way. He knew Money Black didn't know a damn thing about the music business but, to make it look good, he did have a couple of their artists CD's, a few flyers and their managing pamphlet, just in case he wanted to take a look in the briefcase before they got there. Money Black had been completely fooled. He never thought that he could be played out of pocket, and that was exactly what was happening.

"Man! We gon' smash this deal, Smooth! I can feel it," Money Black said as Smooth looked through the rearview mirror at him. He knew what was going to happen and was going right along with the plan. He wanted Money Black out of his mix. It seemed like every day he had to swallow orders given to him by Money Black when, in reality, everything was originally supposed to be in his hands. He was like the Dr. Dre of the south, the way he produced his music, which was really what led Colossal Records to want to strike a deal with G-5 Records in the first place.

"So, what do you think they gon' talk to us about?" Money Black asked him.

"I don't know. This woman is a promotional figure, so she might want to talk to us about shooting some videos for BET or MTV," Smooth said to him.

"That's what's up!" Money Black said, thinking of all the cars that he owned and the girls from the strip club. He reached for his cell phone and tried to call Mitchell, but got no answer.

"Bitch-ass nigga not answering his phone today, huh," he mumbled. He was always used to Mitchell answering his call. He had remembered Mitchell telling him that he needed more work and out of anyone else, Mitchell was probably the one that he would supply first. He was one of his number-one hustlas, plus, he could get him to do anything he told him to.

Smooth flicked the right signal on to exit the freeway. It felt good to see people staring at the big luxury vehicle when they rode by and Money Black was really starting to feel his self.

"Hope she wants my boy Young Thug to work with a big name rapper like Kanye West or Jeezy," Money Black said as he spoke about the guy's talent. Again, Smooth just looked at him through the rearview. They were just around the corner from the place where Javoo and his crew would be waiting.

"Ok, here it is," Smooth said as he noticed Javoo's Range Rover parked next to a 4-door Volvo. Money Black began to check his suit and tie in the back mirror of the Maybach. This was going to be the first time he'd ever met with a major resource outside of the streets.

"You want to do the talkin' or do you want me to?" Smooth asked him.

"Nigga, you the producer, you do the talkin'," Money Black said with authority. Smooth crept the big Maybach slowly into its parking spot, as they noticed a half-black, half-Asian looking woman step out of the door of the place and walk towards the car.

"Damn! She a bad bitch," Money Black said as he watched Stephanie walk towards them. "Hi, my name is Anna Lee, of Colossal Records and Promotions," she said, shaking both of their hands. "You must be Mr. Williams?" she asked Money Black.

"The one and only," he said back to her.

"And you must be Smooth? I've heard a lot about your work," Stephanie said as they walked towards the door of the place. "Oh, and nice car too," she quickly said, trying to make a small conversation.

"Well, thank you, Baby. You know, whenever you wanna ride in it, all you gotta do is just say so," Money Black said with his eyes glued to Stephanie's ass. Stephanie smiled.

"Right this way," she said leading them up a flight of stairs.

"What place is this?" Money Black asked as he observed the antique style of the place.

"It's just a place that a friend from downtown Houston let us use for business meetings." Stephanie said to him.

"Well, I'd like to turn it into a strip club," Money Black said looking up at the ceiling. Stephanie opened the door to a big empty room and walked in.

"Where is everybody?" asked Money Black. A door to the rear of the room came open and that's when Chi-Chi walked in. Smooth's eyes became bucked-wide open at the sight of her, but Money Black couldn't quite figure out who she was. He didn't know her by her face. Then another door opened and Cornelius walked in holding a Glock .9mm. That's when Money Black began to feel nervous.

"What's this here?" he asked, as another door to the room came open and Shalon walked in. Money Black began to nod his head up and down.

"Ok, I see what this is," he said at the sight of her.

"I guess that Javoo is here too? Where the nigga at?" he asked and then hit Smooth upside his head. Javoo walked in the door and stood right behind him.

"I'm right here," he said as Money Black turned to face him. Money Black was already starting to feel that he wasn't going to be leaving this place alive. He immediately swung at Javoo, but he just stepped back to dodge the blow.

"First, you killed Ralph," he said still dodging him.

"And then you kidnapped Shalon and tried to torture her," Javoo said and then caught Money Black in the nose with a jab of his own. Money Black's nose instantly started to bleed. He knew that he was in for a fight, after seeing everyone move to one side of the room. Javoo threw two more jabs, catching him in the jaw and then his chin. That's when Money Black ducked his head and rushed Javoo, scooping him off his feet and slamming him to the floor.

"No, I got him," Javoo said as he saw Cornelius stepped towards them. Cornelius wanted to put that pistol in Money Black's life, but Javoo told him to stand back. They had a plan against Money Black, so Shalon got the keys to his car from Smooth and left the room as he and Javoo tussled on the floor. She ran downstairs and out to Javoo's Range Rover, where she took the duffle bag with the dope and the guns in it and put it in the trunk of Money Black's car. She'd taken the M-5 assault rifle and placed it under the seat in the back and quickly went back inside the place, where Javoo had finally managed to work his way from under Money Black and back to his feet.

"C'mon!" Money Black shouted. He swung at Javoo again, but he side-stepped him and caught him in the ribs.

"You ain't got nothin', Nigga," Javoo said breathing just as heavy as Money Black was. Money Black tried to rush Javoo again but to his surprise, Javoo gave him a knee to the head. He was dazed and lay on the floor with his eyes rolled to the back of his head.

"I could kill you right now," Javoo said as he took the .9mm from Cornelius's hand and put it to his head.

"Wait!" Chi-Chi shouted. "Not before you make him sign these papers," she quickly said, pointing at the X's on the papers.

"Sign this paper or die, Nigga," Javoo gritted his teeth and said as Money Black came to. Smooth took an ink pen out of his pocket and slid it over to him.

"You knew about this the whole time, didn't you?" Money Black said as he looked up at Smooth.

"Sign it, Nigga!" Javoo said, pressing the gun harder to his head. Stephanie stood shocked at what Javoo had done. He had most definitely won her favoritism, as well as a part of her heart. Everything he had told her at the club was true. Money Black was a heartless killer and a ruthless drug dealer and Javoo had taken him single-handedly.

"Now you don't own nothin' but that bullshit-ass car shop, you ho' ass nigga," Javoo said, still pointing the gun at him. There was nothing that Money Black could do. He looked down at his suit. Blood covered his chest.

"This ain't over, Nigga," Money Black said as he picked his car keys up off the floor and looked back at Smooth. He walked out the door with Javoo following behind him.

"You lucky I didn't kill you," Javoo said as he watched Money Black get into his car and leave.

"Chi-Chi, get on your phone and dial 911. Tell' em that you're reporting a man waving a gun in a luxury Maybach with the letters Money B on the license plate, going down the Gulf Freeway," Javoo said as he looked at her. Chi-Chi quickly made the call, while Javoo, Cornelius and Shalon cleaned the blood stains from the floor of the place. Stephanie stood back and looked at Javoo, trying not to let Shalon recognize her attraction to him. It was like she had been star struck and couldn't help herself.

"You are somethin' else," she said as Javoo walked up to her and handed her a brown paper bag.

"Thank you for this," he said and gave her a huge hug. Stephanie took a look inside the bag and then looked back at him. She couldn't say a word after seeing the money in the bag.

"It's $25,000 in case you're wondering," Javoo said. She still didn't know what to say and, for now, all she could do was be grateful.

Chapter Twenty-seven

Money Black furiously drove his car down the Gulf Freeway. He had been dealt with in the worst way as far as he was concerned. His businesses had been burned down, all except one. His money and his drugs had been stolen from him. He had been lied to, tricked and, to say the least, he had been beaten up once again by Javoo.

"That's a'ight," he said to himself as he drove on down 1-45.

"They all gon' pay," he said, talking to himself once more. He drove the Maybach at a high rate of speed, switching from lane to lane, as he ducked in and out of traffic. Suddenly, he looked in his rearview mirror and noticed a baby-blue colored police car with flashing lights duck in behind him.

"D-A-M-N!" he said, not wanting to go through the procedure the man may put him through. He flipped his blinker on and pulled to the side of the freeway. The officer in the police car didn't follow the normal procedure that a cop would usually do. He had pulled to the side of the freeway, just as Money Black had done, but kept a safe distance. Money Black kept his eyes on the rearview. The cop wasn't getting out.

"What this motherfucka doin'?" he said, still waiting for the man to get out. He looked down at his suit. Blood stains were all over him from the busted nose Javoo had given him.

He tried to figure if someone noticed what had happened back at the business mansion and called the police, or that maybe someone thought he mighta stole the $300,000 dollar vehicle. That's when he noticed police cars coming from everywhere on the freeway. They were parking all around him. An unmarked car with dark tinted windows suddenly pulled up in front of him. It was Detective Rollins.

The detective got out with his shooting hand resting on his Glock .40mm as he walked up to Money Black's car. "Mr. Williams, we meet again," he said, noticing his bloody shirt.

"Whatchu want now?" Money Black asked with an attitude.

"Step out of the car, Mr. Williams, and do it slow," said the detective. Money Black opened the door and slowly got out. He began to think about the microwaves, as another police officer had him to spread his legs, while he pat-searched him.

"Mr. Williams, we got a call sayin' that you were seen waving a gun on this here freeway," the detective told him.

"A gun! C'mon man, is that all you can come up with just to have a reason to fuck with me?" he asked the detective.

"Well, I could ask you about the blood on your shirt, but from the looks of your eye, it seems that somebody's been whoopin' yo' ass boy; now that might be a reason you had a gun," the detective said in his own sarcastic fashion.

"Man, I don't got no damn gun," said Money Black.

"So, you're tellin' me that if I look through this car, I won't find a gun? the man asked.

"You can look where you wanna look. I don't got no gun," he repeated.

"Ok Mr. Williams, this is what I'm gon' do for you. I'm gon' have my officer here put you in the back seat of his squad car, while we search your vehicle. If you are clean, then you are free to go," the detective said as Money Black shrugged his shoulders and walked with the officer to his squad car. He wasn't worried at all. He knew his car was clean and would soon be on his way. He sat back in the police car and watched as the detective leaned over inside the Maybach. He had no handcuffs on and so he thought that this would be just another routine stop by the detective. That was what he thought until he began to ask himself why there were so many officers on the scene.

The detective came out with a military issued M-5 assault gun, with a fully loaded clip. Money Black was stunned. The detective smiled as he walked to the trunk of the big luxury car and opened it.

"What the fuck is all that?" Money Black said as the detective pulled out a large duffle bag. He unzipped the bag and to Money Black's surprise, it was full of drugs. Kilo after kilo the man took out of the duffle bag. Then he took out a .12-guage pump shotgun and an AK-47. Money Black knew he was about to be arrested for sure as the detective and the other officer walked back over to the car and opened the door.

"Mr. Williams, you have the right to remain silent," the officer said as he continued to read him his rights. Money Black couldn't believe that this was happening. He had been set up and there was no way that he could prove it. He recognized the kilos and the guns that had been taken from his condo.

"BITCH-ASS-NIGGA!" was all he could say as the officer handcuffed him and helped him get back inside the squad car. The detective stood in the door and looked at him. He shook his head and then began to speak.

"Mr. Williams, we still haven't gotten the test results back on those microwaves, but I can tell you this. We did catch up with your guy Mitchell. He was shot to death and burned to a crisp late last night. You wouldn't happen to know anything about that, would you?" the detective asked him. Money Black just shook his head from side to side as the detective closed the door. One of his number-one hustlers had been found dead but for now he wasn't too concerned about that. He was on his way to jail, and all he could think about was calling his lawyer.

* * *

Chi-Chi felt like a brand new woman. Her mission to find the people who were responsible for her brother's death had finally been completed. She had gotten the record company back and had fallen in love with Cornelius all over again in the process.

"Well, I guess I gotta get y'all money," she said, looking at Cornelius and then at Javoo as they cruised in the Range Rover past Money Black and all the police cars that were sitting on the side of the freeway. Javoo explained to Chi-Chi about the guns and the drugs that he had Shalon put in Money Black's car, which was the reason he had her to make the 911 call.

"We gotta celebrate this," she said as she smiled like never before. Smooth sat next to the door, still amazed at everything that had just happened. But he knew Money Black and he knew that with the type of money that he had, jail wasn't going to hold him.

"So, what we gon' do when he bonds out of jail?" he asked as everyone got silent. The kilos and the hardware would be just enough to hold him, considering the type of money that he had, but Javoo figured that the feds would want to talk to him first.

"Everything is gon' be alright. You just gotta lay low for a couple of days," Javoo told him.

Smooth had planned on doing that anyways, because he knew that Money Black would pay somebody to get him.

"You know we gotta tell Tracy," Shalon said as Javoo looked at her.

"Not yet Baby," he said. He didn't necessarily know how she was gon' feel about them doing what they had done to Mitchell. He knew that she hated him for everything that he had done, but they still needed to give her time to understand what had really happened. He just needed Shalon to stay in her ear to verify her loyalty.

After they all had poured up, given a toast and half-ass celebrated about what had happened to Money Black, Cornelius fired up a blunt and sat back on the sofa in Chi-Chi's apartment. Even he had been caught up in the moment, especially him thinking about his girl having to give him half a million dollars. But he wasn't sure if he should accept the money and asked Javoo what he thought he should do.

249

"Look man, get your money first. Don't let love separate you from no bread. You know the rules, Nigga. But then again, if your heart is telling you that you would be better off by not taking the money, and you believe that, then that's what you need to do. It's your decision," Javoo said as he saw Cornelius put his head down.

"Hey, the girl ain't goin' nowhere man; besides, you all she got, so you better think about that," he said to him.

"You know what? You right, my nig," Cornelius said back to him. The half a million dollars would put him right at the million dollar mark, but staying with Chi-Chi altogether would be worth a lot more. Plus, he really did have feelings for her. Everything he had learned from Javoo had paid off. He had his own place, a couple of nice looking rides, plenty of money, and had not seen the inside of a jail not even once. He had never had a job and it was now time for him to start thinking like a business man. He knew Chi-Chi had several businesses, and he figured that if he couldn't come up with one of his own, she would at least let him have one of hers for himself.

Chapter Twenty-eight

Tracy woke up early the next morning and prepared herself for work. The bruise on her face had finally disappeared as she gently stroked the rim of her eyelid with eye-liner. It felt kinda strange not having Mitchell around but still, she had been disgusted in his actions. She thought about Shalon and wondered if she was going to show up for work today.

"Let me call her," she said, picking up her phone.

"Hello," answered Shalon.

"You comin' to work today?" Tracy asked her.

"Yeah, I'll be there," she said.

"So, whatcha been doin'?" Tracy asked.

"Girl, I gotta tell you all about it," Shalon said to her.

"What, about Mitchell?" she asked.

"Yeah! I'll talk to you about it at work, ok?" Shalon said to her.

"Ok then, see you at the job," Tracy said and then hung up.

* * *

Money Black sat in a holding cell, wondering what was taking his lawyer so long to bail him out. His bond really had not yet been set and he was getting frustrated. He felt like his lawyer was the best in town, and one who could come thru at any cost.

"Do we have a Mr. Eric Williams in here?" a sheriff's deputy asked as he stood at the door of the holding cell. Money Black stood up and walked to the door.

"Your attorney is here, so follow me," the jailer said. After all the money he had given the man, it was about time, he thought. He had been in jail all night long, he'd still had on his bloody suit and he was ready to get out of it.

"Damn man! What's the fuckin' hold up? I been in here since yesterday afternoon," Money Black said as he sat at the glass window in the visitation area and looked at his lawyer.

"We got some complications with getting you out," his lawyer told him.

"Whatchu mean, complications?" Money Black asked him.

"The judge is not going to give you a bond because of the guns and the drugs they found in your car," the lawyer said.

"Why not? That's what I pay you for - to get me a bond," said Money Black.

"Well, one of the guns found in your car matches the ballistics report of a guy that was found shot and burned almost beyond recognition while he was still in his car. The feds have recommended that you get no bond, considering the amount of drugs that you had, plus the type of hardware that was found in your car. They say you have too much money and they don't want to take the chance of you being a flight risk. They're investigating the guy's murder as we speak," his lawyer said as he put his head into the palm of his hands.

"They want to charge you with conspiracy to first degree murder, possession of illegal firearms and aggravated possession of a controlled substance," the man told him. Money Black ran his fingers back and forth over his head. Not only had Javoo beat him, he had also masterminded a way to hang a hook in him.

"Look man! I been set up. Look at my suit," he said to his lawyer. Even though he had explained everything that had happened, it was hard for him to come up with any names. He didn't know Javoo's real name and he couldn't mention Shalon's name because of the kidnapping. He couldn't mention Chi-Chi's name because of what she knew about the murder of her brother and his wife. He was stuck between a rock and a hard spot and now, the only deals he would be able to make from this point on would be in a courtroom.

EPILOGUE

Chi-Chi and Smooth sat in the back of the club, while Young Thug celebrated the release of his new album. They had shot a video earlier that day, courtesy of Colossal Records, as his single sat at number 3 on the billboards.

"I think everything is gon' be alright," Smooth said as he threw his arm around Chi-Chi.

"Yeah, it's what my brother woulda wanted," she said, looking up at him. Chi-Chi was now considered a top-notch chick in Smooth's book. Her swag had seemed powerful to him and just on the strength of her brother, he gave her his loyalty.

Shalon and Tracy ended up quitting the job they both worked in the Galleria Mall and started "Ladies First", their own fashion boutique, on the other side of town. Shalon continued to stay loyal to Javoo, as well as Tracy, about Mitchell's murder. Thanks to Javoo, their bank accounts didn't look too bad either.

Stephanie, Marissa and Laura continued to party every so often. Stephanie had grown to like Javoo in a way she had never imagined and would soon find herself in a lustful need for him.

Javoo and Cornelius remained on low-key status, as they continued their reign on the streets. They were always on the prowl to hit major licks. Javoo and his wife Tanasia had found some land on the outskirts of Houston and had their dream home built, while Cornelius and Chi-Chi did the same. They were now engaged to be married as well.

Money Black ended up getting 40 years in the federal penitentiary. He had spent most of his money on lawyers and trying to fight off the district attorney, who was pushing for the death penalty for Mitchell's murder. He was sent to a federal facility in Florida, where he sat at the back of his cell with only one person on his mind: Javoo, the Bona Fide Street Thug.

THE END.

EXCERPT FROM BOOK 2 of the BONAFIDE STREET
THUG TRILOGY

STREET WORK

By Donald Ray Johnson

Chapter One

"That's what I do baby, I work the streets," Cornelius said
to one of his homies, as they high-capped at each other, after
the guy saw a girl give him some money out of her purse.
Cornelius had made a quick bet with the girl, after Larry
Fitzgerald ran a 45 yard touchdown against the Pittsburgh
Steelers.

It was like the 2008-2009 Super bowl all over again and
Cornelius was a huge Pittsburgh fan. Everyone had been on
their toes when Pittsburgh's defense forced a fumble and
recovered the ball with only a minute left in the game. The girl
had been somewhat eyeballing him already and when he and
his homie made their bets, he locked eyes with her and asked
if she wanted to bet too, since she screamed so loudly in his
ear when the Cardinals scored.

The sports bar they were in was crowded. They had free
crawfish and $2 dollar specials on drinks. Mostly everyone
there were working people, except for maybe a few dough-

boys, who were on their grind in the streets. The parking lot
was full with all kinds of whips, making the valet section a
real life car show.

"Hey, I didn't mean to take your money," Cornelius said, as
he walked up to the girl he made the bet with and attempted to
giver her back the $20 bill she had given him.

"Oh no! A bet is a bet," the girl said as she turned to him,
surprised that he came to her.

"Hi, my name is Cornelius," he said, waving to the bartender.

"My name is Rene," she said."

"At least let me buy you a drink with this. I don't want you
to think that all I do is go around taking money from women,"
he said as he smiled sarcastically.

"That's okay. I'm gon' get you back," she said.

"Whatchu like to drink?" he asked, as the bartender
snapped his fingers to the sound of the order she made.

"Pink Panties, huh? So, is that what you have on now?" he
asked as he profiled next to her.

"Maybe I do, maybe I don't," she said and then gave him a
sarcastic smile of her own. "Where are you from and whatchu
do for a livin'?" she asked.

"I'm from right here in Houston and I own and run my own
detail shop. What about you?" he asked her back.

"I'm from Houston. I work in the medical center," she told
him.

"So, if I collapse right now, would you give me mouth-to-
mouth?" Cornelius jokingly asked. Rene smiled. Cornelius
had turned her on, just as he could do almost any girl.

"I would do anything to help someone stay alive," she said to him. Another girl came over and stood next to Rene. She had been using the restroom and was now eye-ballin' him like he had committed a crime.

"So who is this, one of your friends?" he asked as he looked at the new girl.

"Yes, and we're about to leave, so I'm going to give you my number. Call me, okay?" Rene said as she quickly wrote down her number on a napkin, gave it to him and then she and the other girl left.

Cornelius looked at the number and smiled.

"As usual," he said as he downloaded the girl's number into his cell phone. He looked over towards the entrance and saw two Puerto Rican girls walk in."

"Daaaamn!" he said, as his face frowned at the sight of their bodies. One of the girls looked like she came right out of a Smooth Girl Magazine and the other, a Show. Behind them stood two Latino-looking guys, who appeared to be their boyfriends. They looked over in his direction and then decided to go to the bar. Cornelius stood there, as they walked towards him and then stopped to order some drinks.

"What's up?" Cornelius said, shortly throwing his head up, after noticing that one of the guys was checking him out.

"What's up Homies?" the Latino guy asked. The first guy looked sorta like Daddy Yankee. He wore a diamond necklace that looked to be worth at least a hundred grand and a diamond bracelet. He had on a pair of Marc Jacobs sun shades and an Ed Hardy hook up. The other guy was dressed almost the same, except he was taller and his hair was longer

"Hey man, you know where I can get somethin' to smoke?" the first guy asked him.   Cornelius gave him a sincere look.

"Whatcha lookin' for, some Reggie Bush?' Cornelius asked, hitting him with the street talk.

"Nah man! I'm lookin' for that George Bush," the guy said, high-fiving the other guy as they laughed. Cornelius didn't sense that they were police working undercover, so he thought that he'd give 'em a joog.

"Are y'all new in town or somethin'? You look like you the man. You should already be on," he said speaking at the guy's swag.

"Yeah, we new in town. Just got here yesterday," he said."

"Y'all just visiting or what?" Cornelius asked.

"Nah, we here to stay. We're about to be Houstonians," the guy said to him.

"OK, that's what's up," Cornelius said back to him. Cornelius wore a black Roca Wear sleeveless bomber over a white long-sleeve Roca Wear shirt and black Roca Wear denim jeans. He wore a Cartier Rolex watch and a diamond dog-tag necklace that he had Johnny Dang design. He even had on his favorite pinky ring, that sparkled every time he took a sip of his drink, which the girls noticed whenever he moved his hand.

"You seem like a cool cat. I just might turn you on," Cornelius said, looking at him. The guy whispered something in Spanish to the girls they were with, then told Cornelius that he wanted to go outside.

"So what y'all ridin' in?" Cornelius asked as the guy pointed over to a Mercedes G550 SUV.

"OK, I see you clean," he told him. These guys didn't appear to be no scrubs, he thought. Their appearance, the girls they were with and what they were riding in told him that they were ballers.

"Whatchu drive?" the guy asked Cornelius. He pointed over to a bronze-colored Aston Martin sitting next to a Jag. His wife Chi-Chi had given him the car for his birthday, shortly after they were married. She had had the car since her brother had been killed by a ruthless drug dealer from the north side of town, and knew that he had a serious crush on the ride. He unlocked the door, reached into the console and grabbed a sack of purple haze hydro marijuana.

"Come on, let's go sit in my ride," the guy said and then they walked over to the Benz G-Wagon and got in.

"So what's your name homey?" Cornelius asked the guy.

"My name is Daniel and that's my cousin, Carlos," Daniel said, and then reached back to shake his hand.

"So what's the deal with y'all bein' new in town?" Cornelius asked as he twisted up a blunt and then fired it up.

"My uncle just left me a fuckin' cleaners, man. So me and my people came down from the Big Apple to see what it do, you know what I mean?" Daniel said to him.

"What happened to him?" Cornelius asked, blew out some smoke and then passed him the blunt.

"He was killed down near the border in a drug war between two different drug cartels," said Daniel. Daniel and his wife Sofia had lived out in Brooklyn, New York ever since they first met. His mother and father had moved from Puerto Rico to Brooklyn when he was only a baby and what a time it was for him as a kid. He grew up fast, helping his dad run a restaurant when he was only a teenager . His mom had suddenly grown sick and his father was needing money badly, so he and his cousin Carlos started peddling drugs in the alley behind his father's restaurant. He had started to make way more money than his father was making, and at the age of 18, he bought himself a Lexus just to satisfy his hustle. That's when his uncle came to visit and suddenly noticed him. He gave him tips on how to strive in the game. By the time he was 21, he was getting his own shipments from someone his uncle knew out in Manhattan. That was what put him and his cousin on another level. He knew he had to take in the family and just before his mom died, she'd told him that his father was starting to come down with Alzheimer's and for him to take care of his two sisters. And so, Daniel made a promise to her that he would.

"OK, I'm Cornelius," he said returning his introduction. He watched as Carlos stuck his hand in his pocket and came out with a small Zip-Lock baggie. He stuck two fingers in the bag and pulled out a pill.

"I see you like that x homey," Cornelius said to him.

"Yeah, I cut for them Blue Dolphins, you want one?" he asked him.

"Nah, I'm cool, homey," said Cornelius.

After they finished smoking the blunt they got out and went back inside the sports bar. Daniel's two sisters were surrounded by a rowdy group of college frat brothers, and as they walked through the crowded group of people, the crowd began to break up .

"My sisters are always flirting and drawing too much attention," Daniel said, looking at Cornelius.

"Your sisters!" Cornelius said, with a surprised look on his face.

Daniel began to introduce the girls to him. "This is my sister Lorena and this is Margarita," he said as Cornelius looked at them.

"Hi!" they both said, giving him a short wave. Cornelius hung out around the sports bar a lot longer than he expected, flossing and making eyes with Daniel's sister, Margarita. He had promised his wife Chi-Chi that he would come home a lot earlier than the past two nights, after he and his main man, Javoo, had done some of their own surveillance on a guy that Javoo had heard about, and one that was making some major moves in the streets. That's when his cell phone began to ring. It was Javoo.

"Yeah, what's up?" he said as he answered Javoo's call.

"I just got the OK on this sucka man. It's time for some action," Javoo told him. Cornelius hung up the phone. He really didn't want to leave, but he had to.

"OK, fellas, I gotta burn. Y'all stay up," Cornelius said, as he looked at Rita and began to walk away. "Hey, hold up. Let me getcha number before you go," Daniel said to him. Cornelius and Daniel quickly exchanged numbers. He had some work to do and so he threw up the duce at Rita, turned and left the bar.

Javoo drove his new Chevy Camaro down Cullen Boulevard, as he thought about all the times he'd told his wife Tanasia, that he was going to quit the streets. His son Javon had just recently turned 10 and was now playing on a little league football team. His daughter Natasia, was now eight years old and had become a very good dancer to his imagination, as he smiled at the thought of her in front of him and Tanasia, trying to perform a skit Beyonce had done during the BET Awards. That's when his cell phone suddenly began to ring. It was Cornelius.

"What's up?" he said as he answered.

"I had to go change cars. What's the deal?" he asked.

"Man, this dude we been watchin', he owns a late night bar. I have somebody there now, keepin' an eye on him, while we go check his spot out on 1-45 and Scarsdale. He's suppose to have a couple hundred G's stashed in the attic. We need to get that. His 17-year-old son is suppose to be the only one there, so hurry up and meet me at the sky rise," Javoo told him.

"OK," Cornelius said and then hung up. Cornelius still had Chi-Chi's old sky-rise apartment over in the Galleria area. He had given up his spot over in Holly Hall, after they had their home built out in Pearland and now used the apartment as a meeting place for whenever he and Javoo made moves. It was already around twelve o'clock midnight and Javoo had to figure out a way to get in that house. That's when he thought about his number two sweetheart, Shalon.

Shalon lay dead asleep in her bed. She had worked all day and had stayed up fairly late, hoping that Javoo would come over, but he had other plans. They had been seeing each other for several years now and she was still very much in love with him. Shalon, who was now 26 years old, still looked a lot younger and could easily pass for a 19 or 20 year old, which was exactly what Javoo needed to get the young kid to open the door without them having to kick it in.

Her phone began to ring, as she tossed and turned before answering it, trying to shake off the sleep that had her body lifeless.

"Hello," she said finally answering the all.

"Get up. I need you right now," Javoo said to her.

"OK, whatchu want me to do and whatchu want me to wear?" she asked as she sat up on her bed and turned on her night lamp. She had grown accustomed to Javoo's ways and the things that he did. She had finally came to the conclusion that she was never going to get him to leave his wife, and so doing whatever he asked always turned out to be profitable in her book, especially when it came to something like this.

"I need you to wear somethin' skimpy. Maybe be a short skirt and some heels. I gotta 17- year-old kid at home alone and we need to get him to answer the door. You know the routine," Javoo said to her. Shalon had become a very good actress as well. She done all kinds of things. She'd once pretended to be a cheerleader for the Houston Rockets and had persuaded a wealthy drug dealer into taking her home with him, only to set it up so that Javoo and Cornelius could rob him; then another time she'd pretended to be a Hurricane

Katrina evacuee, needing a job and a place to stay, when a wealthy Columbian guy offered to take her in, thinking that he could get some sex, and that's when Javoo and Cornelius came in to rob him as well.

"You know where to meet me and hurry up, we only got about a good hour to put this work in," Javoo said and then hung up. Shalon threw on something simple, but it was also sexy. She'd thought that, the kid was only 17, so waking him out of his sleep would be like a dream to him once he saw her.

Javoo looked at his watch, wondering when Shalon was going to show up. It was a quarter to one and he wanted to have this job done before a quarter to two.

"C'mon baby-girl," he said aloud as he and Cornelius sat in his Range Rover waiting on her. Just then, the headlights of her Chrysler 300 pulled into the parking garage.

"Damn, it's about time," he said as she got out and skipped her way over to the Range Rover and got in the back seat.

"You ready?" she asked as Javoo checked out her appearance. Shalon was a very sexy dark-skinned chick. She would remind you of Chili, from the group TLC, whenever you saw her. She wore a very short Coogi denim skirt and glass bottom heels, with red leather straps that were up to her calves. She had on a tight red short-sleeve Coogi top and red lipstick. Her hair was pulled back into a pony tail and she wore a set of delicious-looking hoop earrings with red diamonds in them.

"I thought I said the boy was only seventeen," Javoo said, feeling like she had over- dressed. Cornelius immediately started to laugh.

267

"Shut up Cornelius!" she said, as Javoo put the SUV in reverse and headed out towards Scarsdale.

It was about 1:15 a.m. when Shalon, along with Javoo and Cornelius got out of the Range Rover across the street from the house that they wanted to invade. The neighborhood they were in was a pretty legit place. Javoo knew they couldn't be seen doing anything that looked suspicious, for fear of any of the neighbors calling the police. But it was dark, the timing was right and the front door of the house sat back in a space between the garage and the living room, so they had no other choice but to give it a try.

Shalon rang the doorbell constantly. Ten minutes had passed and the boy still had not answered the door. Now Javoo was thinking about just kicking the door in, but the light above the door all of a sudden came on. Shalon could tell that someone was looking through the peep-hole, as she turned and looked back in Javoo's direction. The lock on the door clicked and the door finally came open. It was the 17-year-old boy.

"Yeah, what's up?" the kid asked, rubbin' his eyes with his hand.

"Um, I'm sorry if I woke you up, but my car won't start and I'm tryin' to get back to the southwest side. My cell phone died. Could I use your phone to call somebody to come get me?" she asked as the boy looked at her with amazement. He didn't look much like a 17-year-old kid at all. He was tall, standing nearly six foot three, and was already growing a mustache.

"Yeah, yeah! Come on in," the boy said. He had opened the door up wide, so that Shalon could walk in past him, when

Javoo and Cornelius ran from the darkness, pointing their guns at him.

"Get down, get down!" Javoo said, grabbing the boy and forcing him down to the floor, while Cornelius closed the door.

"Wait! Who is y'all?" the boy tried to ask, as Cornelius quickly began to duct tape him. "Just be quiet kid and everything will be ok," Javoo said, assuring the boy of his safety.

Javoo and Shalon walked to the hallway and headed upstairs, where they found the entrance to the attic, while Cornelius searched the bottom level of the house. Once they went into the attic, Javoo pulled a small flashlight out of his pocket and began to shine it throughout the attic. Over in the corner of the attic, he could see six boxes that were sealed with tape. Quickly, he took a fancy-looking butterfly knife from his pocket, flipped it open and jabbed one of the boxes, splitting it from side to side. He opened the cardboard lid and saw nothing but stacks of hundreds, so he grabbed the other boxes and split them open one at a time as well.

"This what I'm talkin' bout right here," he said nodding his head.

"But we gotta find a way to get 'em to the Range without making so many trips back and forth to the house " he quickly said. Shalon quickly turned and went down to one of the rooms in the house. She returned with a couple of bed sheets that she'd found in the hamper.

"Here, let's pour three boxes in one and three in the other," she said, spreading one of the sheets out over the floor. Javoo began to dump the boxes of money out onto the sheet and then quickly tied the ends together. He took the knife, cut the other three boxes open and began to pour them out onto the second sheet as well. When he opened the last and final box, it came to his surprise what he saw inside. It was filled with bags of diamonds, very colorful rubies, emeralds and solid gold coins, that seemed to be from another country. He sat that box to the side and quickly tied the ends of the second sheet together.

"Let's get back downstairs," he said as he picked the box of jewels up, put it onto his shoulders and then reached down to grab the first sheet, while Shalon picked up the second.

It didn't take them but a few seconds to get back down to where Cornelius was standing guard over the boy they had duct-taped on the floor.

"Let's go," he said as he handed Cornelius the sheet loaded with money. Shalon struggled with the sheet that she was carrying. She walked in a criss-cross pattern, as the loaded sheet of money bounced around on her back, nearly knocking her to the floor.

"Here girl! Carry this," Javoo said, handing her the box. He grabbed the sheet by the knot, threw it over his shoulder, stepped over the kid and then walked out of the front door, with Cornelius and Shalon following behind him.

It was just about two o'clock in the morning, as they headed back down the freeway, when Cornelius' phone suddenly began to ring.

"Hey Baby," he said as he answered.

"Where are you?" his wife Chi-Chi asked.

"I'm out takin' care of some business. I'll be home in a little while," he told her.

"Are you with Javoo?"' she asked.

"Yes, I am, so go to bed baby. Everythin's cool," he said to her.

Chi-Chi wasn't going to argue that. Even though she had once asked him to stop doing what he was doing, she knew that as long as Javoo was in the picture he would be OK, especially when there was some money involved.

About the Author

Author Donald Ray Johnson is one who has seen and done it all. After being sentenced on a felony drug charge, he was sent to a Texas state prison, where he discovered his own ability to write street fiction.

Donald is looking to be released soon and will continue to lead Southern Classic Publishing with the release of "Street Work", a second novel from the Bona Fide Street Thug trilogy. Be on the look out for work he has done in other fields of the literary world, which will also be released in the near future.

See more at: http://southernclassicpublishing.com/scp-authors/donald-ray-johnson/

Book Order Form

Please print this form and mail with your check or money order, payable to:

Southern Classic Publishing
990 Hwy 287 N Ste 106 # 298
Mansfield TX, 76063
682-587-9818

Web: www.SouthernClassicPublishing.com
Email: SouthernClassicPublishing@gmail.com

Books will be mailed through regular postal mail media. Delivery may require 2- 3 weeks.

Quantity	Book Title	Cost	Total
	Bona Fide Street Thug	14.95	
Add	U.S Add $4, Outside US $10 Shipping & Handling per book		
	Total Submitted		

Ship to
Name_____

Address_____

City State and Zip_____

Telephone/Email Address_____

Thank you for your business!

55249757R00159

Made in the USA
Charleston, SC
21 April 2016